To my dear
Linda
Thank for your encouraging
words always.
Love ♡
Janet Morris Belvin
October 3, 2021

THE

Refuge

Also by Janet Morris Belvin:

Southern Stories from the Porch Swing

THE

Refuge

a novel

JANET MORRIS BELVIN

Print ISBN: 978-1-66780-0-196
eBook ISBN: 978-1-66780-0-202

Cover art by Jerry Morris Hester

BookBaby Publishers
Printed in the United States of America.

Dedication

For all of you who have ever encouraged me and recommended my writing, for every English teacher I ever had, for librarians and booksellers everywhere who recommend this book, for Emily (who didn't arrive in time to make it into my last book) and as always for you, Paul.

And for Mama, Daddy and Camden – ever in my heart.

Acknowledgments

As a young girl, growing up in Savannah, GA, I spent many hours in the children's section of the Savannah Public Library, a grand granite structure on Bull Street. There under the tutelage of Children's Librarian Miss May McCall, I was introduced to the magic of the printed page. Books gave me then as they do now entrée into other worlds, other personas, other occupations which I would never have been able to see or do on my own. So I read…and read…and eventually I began to write.

This novel is the product of, literally, several years' work. But, in addition to being the result of the hours I've spent in front of a blank computer screen, hoping and praying for inspiration, I also owe a lot to everyone who has helped me along the path to publication. As always, I first want to thank Paul, without whose belief in me I could not have proceeded. My sisters Louise Purdy, Martha Jean Cooke, and Jerry Hester (my twin) have been supportive throughout the process. My children, Tom, Julie, Katherine, Shon, Caroline and Ben have given me such joy (and occasionally some material for the book.) Derry Stockbridge, another Georgia author, gave me initial helps when I was just starting.

I'd also like to thank several friends who gave me so much encouragement when I was deciding whether or not to write: Deanna Wright Marsh; My Savannah friends: Polly Powers Stramm (who gave me some much needed publicity in her *Savannah Morning News* column,) Lynn Platt

Hagan, Joe Berry, Muriel Rabhan Varon and Nancy Asher Bracker (the Divas), Cliff McCurry, John Broderick, Ginger Price Masingill, Terri Bell Hulsey, Beth Everette, and Johnny Roach (for valuable information about the aircraft;) One Lap friends: Jonathan Biven and his mom Nancy, Carol Waldron Burke, and Janet Rice; My Gates County friends: Rita Lane, Dette Buck, Pat Familiar, Phyllis Hobbs, Renee Hinton McGinnis, and Bessie Hinton, and Emmaline Umphlett (whose name I used because I love it so); My Meredith Angels: Cindy Griffith McEnery (always) Susan Soloway Daul, Cathy Winstead, Sue Hammons Cook, Molly Beck, Jane A. DeVos, and Betty A. Harrington; My Langston Hughes buddies: Byron Cotton and Colleen Smith; My Raleigh friends: Billie Freeman, Martha Goodson, Margie Mearns; My Gaffney friends: Nancy Clarkson Fowler, Tim Gibson, and Sally Turner Grindstaff; My cousin Ursula Luckett and so many others.

And for all the rest of you whose names I have forgotten to add. (Sooo sorry!) and those who bought this book – I offer you my sincerest thank you.

Love,

Janet

XOXO

Contents

Prologue:

The Funeral

PEYTON THURMAN PICKED UP A CLOD OF BLACK VIRGINIA soil, squeezed it in her hands tightly and tossed it into the combined gravesites of her mother and father. Rubbing her hands together to shed the dirt, she looked up. The skies above were grey and sodden, matching her mood. She stood a moment and looked down into the opening, now containing the coffins of her parents, and wiped a tear from her eye. Rain came down in a steady drip, mirroring the tears she could not control. Standing around the grave were a hundred or so people, their faces hidden behind rainbow colored umbrellas. At the head of the grave beneath a funeral home tent, the minister stood and read the 23rd Psalm. He offered a long prayer but Peyton couldn't focus. She looked out toward the horizon, past the tiny stone church nearby, and wondered, *"Now what?"*

Peyton's parents, Jimmy and Dorothy Thurman, a wealthy farmer/businessman and his wife, had been on the way to Louisville, Kentucky and the Kentucky Derby in the single engine Cessna that Jimmy piloted on weekends. An examination by the National Transportation Safety Board revealed that wind shears due to the unpredictable weather of a late spring storm had caused the plane to go down over the mountains of West Virginia. This at least gave Peyton some comfort as Jimmy was always diligent about maintaining all of his vehicles and equipment so it could not have been human error. When both husband and wife were killed instantly, the West Virginia State Police working the scene gathered all the contents of the plane's cabin. Among the findings was Peyton's business card in Dorothy's wallet. The police used it to make the sad call to her as soon as the bodies were recovered. Peyton, at 32, unmarried and an editor for Oxford University Press in London, had received the news while at work and her supervisor had insisted she take off immediately for the United States. So Peyton had gone home at once to Virginia to settle the somewhat convoluted estates of her father and mother.

Now she stood at the yawning grave which held her parents' bodies and looked at the crowd in attendance. She knew all of these people from her childhood here. All of them would go home tonight to houses full of people, loved ones to cherish, and jobs to do. She would go home to her parents' farm, to Greyson, all alone.

At the end of the graveside service, people came up to her offering hugs and sentiments. *Just let us know what we can do, Hon. We're bringing some fried chicken. Call us if you need anything.* Peyton nodded grimly, trying to smile and say thank you. But she knew that she was really on her own. She walked back to the limousine which would take her back to the funeral home. She'd take care of paying for her parents' funeral and then figure out what to do next.

At the same time, five miles down the road, a dusty farm truck maneuvered down a back lane of the Greyson property. The sun was below the horizon and shadows engulfed a large ramshackle barn and its surroundings ahead. Slowing his vehicle to a stop, the driver put the truck in park and got out. He headed for the old barn, looking to the left and right to see if he had been spotted. Following him were two men who wore ball caps pulled low over their stubbled faces. They spoke in grunts and heavily accented whispers.

"This oughta be just fine. Unload this truck and hurry up," the driver told the two men. "I don't want anyone to see us. Put it all right over there," he added, pointing to a dark corner of the barn.

The two laborers proceeded to unload household equipment and chemicals. explosives, solvents, metals, salts, and corrosives into various wheelbarrows and tractor-drawn carts while the driver watched nervously. The men stacked the items in what was an ever-growing pile of similar items in the far corner of the barn amidst shadows and cobwebs.

"Hey, be careful," the driver cautioned. "That stuff is worth a lot. And one word of this to anybody and that money you owe me comes due tomorrow, you hear?"

"Yeah, *si*" the men grunted in reply and continued unloading.

The airport was crowded with people headed to all parts of the world. One day after her parents' funeral, Peyton moved past the ticketing agent heading for Gate 11. She stopped to check the departure status of her flight, and then moved swiftly to the security screening station. To her left and right, children pulled at their parents' legs crying for something. Distracted business travelers rushed ahead, their cellphones glued to their ears. Pilots and flight attendants walked purposefully toward their gates, pulling neat wheeled travel bags behind them. She walked through the metal detector, raising her arms when told to do so. Collecting her bags after their trip through the x-ray machine, she followed the signs to her flight's gate area. Once there, she showed her boarding pass to the attendant and boarded a British Airways jet bound for London Heathrow Airport out of Dulles. Her head was full of things she had to accomplish in the next few weeks.

She settled herself into the cushioned leather of the first class cabin seat and tucked her bag under the seat in front of her. Nervously, she buckled the seat belt and looked around to see her fellow passengers. The flight attendant cheerily approached her and offered her a bottle of chilled water and warm cookies which Peyton refused.

"No, thank you," she said softly. "Maybe later."

She closed her eyes and leaned her head back on the seat. She'd been making mental lists of all she had to do for days. Now the time had come to act on them.

"There's nothing to do but take a leave of absence from my job and move back here," she thought. *"There's no way I'll ever get everything done right any other way."*

The plane's engines ramped up and Peyton steeled herself for the nerves she always felt at takeoff. An uneasy flier at the best of times, Peyton squeezed her eyes shut and prayed for peace. She clasped and unclasped her hands and waited for the flight attendant's familiar spiel. A tear leaked from her eye and she wiped it away quickly.

No time for that now, she told herself. *Here we go.*

The flight was uneventful, allowing her to take a couple of catnaps. When the plane landed right on time, she breathed a sigh of relief. Peyton gathered her belongings and looked out the tiny plane window to the misty skies above London. One half hour later, after collecting her luggage at the baggage carousel, she walked through the terminal past duty-free shops, lounges and passengers racing to make a connection at another gate. Finally stepping out into the light rain of a London morning, she hailed a taxi - cab, handed her bags to the cabbie and gave him her address. Then settling back into the seat of the black cab, she closed her eyes and tried not to think.

Chapter One:

London One Last Time

PEYTON TURNED THE KEY IN THE DOOR OF HER LONDON FLAT and struggled to bring her suitcases over the threshold. On the windowsill, the one African violet she had attempted to grow had thrown in the towel, the leaves brown and crackly, and the once pink petals of the plant were now lying lifeless on the floor. She rolled her suitcases to the bedroom and tossed them carelessly on the bed. She opened her closet and rolled her eyes. The clothes within were hardly suitable for life on a Virginia farm which is where she'd be for the foreseeable future. Hanging on the bar were business suits that fit perfectly her life as a successful editor. Tailored pantsuits and Dupioni silk dresses which she had worn to important publishing events were completely wrong for what was ahead of her. Peyton had finally decided on the flight from Virginia that she would have to take some time off to settle her parents' estate.

As soon as she'd taken off her suit jacket, Peyton kicked her heels off and pulled her cellphone from her pocket. Scrolling through the list of contacts, she found the number of her supervisor, calling him while she still had the nerve.

Before she could get out a "hello," Laird Duncan, welcomed her back and with the smooth diplomacy for which he was known, offered her a six-month leave of absence.

"But. Laird, I'm still in negotiations with the Broad Camden children's book author for our fall catalogue. We were supposed to meet next week to interview several artists."

"Not to worry, Peyton," he replied. "We've got this. You just take care of yourself right now. From what I know of your parents' farm, just getting that settled will take months. "

Laird and his wife had visited the Thurmans when they were in New York City for a publishing convention. Peyton had flown home at the same time and invited them to visit her parents' estate. The Duncans had been thoroughly charmed by Jimmy and Dorothy.

"Well, if you're sure...I appreciate the consideration, Laird."

And just that fast, she decided to take the leave. Almost immediately, her brain began making lists of what she'd need to do before returning to Virginia. She thought for a minute, then took nearly half the clothes off the clothes rack and piled them in a chair.

"I'll donate some of these," she thought, "or just toss them. There'll be no need for them at Greyson. "

She began carefully folding her city clothes, once so beloved, into boxes and bags and labeled them for donation. She was pulling the last silk blouse off the hanger when her cellphone buzzed. It was a text from a number she didn't recognize. It had a Virginia area code so she assumed it was someone she knew.

"Looking forward to talking with you about your plans.
Will call when you get in. – Cameron. "

Chapter Two:

Greyson

Far BACK FROM THE TWO-LANE HIGHWAY THAT CUT THROUGH the rolling hills of northern Virginia, the house had stood on a bluff overlooking a tributary of the Potomac River since colonial times. Constructed of red brick laid in Flemish bond, Greyson claimed three stories and a full basement when it was constructed in 1722. Thomas Grey and his pretty young bride Louisa occupied it soon after its completion. Their plantation was extensive and included this large, handsome dwelling placed jewel-like amidst a setting of numerous outbuildings.

Grey had been born in 1699 in the small mill village of Blockley, Gloucestershire, in England, the son of John Grey, a poor miller and his wife. Hearing practically daily reports of the Colonies, John determined to seek his fortune there and escape the drudgery of the mill. So he put aside his earnings for a year, sold what few possessions he had and booked passage to America on an East Indiaman ship carrying cargo to the American colonies. Disembarking in Hampton in 1701, he made his way with his wife and tiny son to the area of Virginia which was to become Loudoun County. There John, with his wife Bertha and their son Thomas, established a trading post on land he bought from the natives.

Thomas, an only child, grew up to be handsome, spoiled and impulsive, coddled by his mother. As far as Bertha was concerned, Thomas could do no wrong and she frequently took his side in the constant arguments between John and his son. As soon as he reached manhood, Thomas left home and went to sea. Initially, he endured the cramped conditions of the ship he hired onto as well as the bad weather and low pay that came with being an able seaman. Still, he soon he found that he had a natural affinity for the sea and, before too long, aided by the monies he'd acquired from gambling, he was captain of a small sailing vessel of his own. He earned his fortune by chartering ships and ferrying goods from Europe to the colonies and then exporting tobacco from his father John Grey's wharf to England. By 1722, he had acquired enough capital to construct the stately house which was to be known as Greyson. He spared no expense in the construction of the mansion with its simple, classic lines and graceful proportions.

On one of his visits to Grey's Wharf from London, he happened to meet the girl who would become his wife, Louisa Bond. A beautiful, slender brunette with intelligence and grit, she fell in love with Thomas almost as soon as they were introduced. As Thomas's house neared completion, he proposed to Louisa and she accepted immediately. They were married in the yard of his parents' small trading post nearby and Thomas began ordering furnishings for the house from England – silver teapots and flatware engraved with their initials, a mahogany table and twelve chairs, carved four-poster beds and richly colored Oriental carpets, all to please Louisa. Thomas's love for Louisa was fierce and once, in the heat of passion, he had scratched his name and that of his bride in the glass of a dining room window. The year 1723 was carved underneath. Then he'd presented the diamond he'd used as a carving tool to Louisa, a token of his love.

But, Thomas was well-known for his hot temper, his taste for gambling on horses and his propensity for drunkenness. A short five years after his 1723 wedding, in a fit of drunken pride, Grey bet the entire two thousand acre estate with its crops of tobacco and corn and its mansion, 50 slaves and 10,000 pounds in ready cash on a race between his grey Arabian stallion and a bright chestnut Thoroughbred from a farm in nearby Fauquier County. The grey pulled up lame after the first turn on the dirt track and everything Grey owned was gone in a moment. Grey was distraught and returned to Greyson to tell his wife what had transpired. Two weeks later he had loaded several wagons with furniture and clothing and headed to Grey's Station, the trading post his parents had established nearby. Wordlessly, he and Louisa began unloading the few possessions they had brought with them. Louisa rolled up her sleeves and began cleaning the long-empty log building where John and Bertha had first lived upon coming to America. Meanwhile, Thomas sat on a tree stump outside dreaming of another, much grander home to take the place of Greyson's Wharf. He decided he'd call it The Refuge.

Years later, Thomas and Louisa inherited the trading post from John and Bertha upon their deaths, John from a stroke and Bertha from a heart attack not long after. . Determined to rebuild his fortune, Thomas worked day and night to enlarge the trading post and the contents of his purse. Soon he was able to buy back one thousand of the original two thousand acres of the Greyson property, but hadn't enough capital to purchase the manor house as he wanted. It sat empty while Thomas and Louisa, childless and middle-aged, moved into the house Thomas had built to replace Greyson.

The Refuge sat on a hillside promontory, giving a view of the river below. At first, the approach to the house was by river traffic, but soon, as Thomas began exploring the forests surrounding his land, he discovered footpaths made over centuries by the Native Americans who had roamed the area. Thomas and other colonists began to use these paths which naturally became the roads to take goods to market. Realizing the availability of such a road some distance from The Refuge, Thomas graded a long drive stretching from the house to the road. He planted a series of young oaks equally spaced on either side of the drive and watered them faithfully. Thomas began to be a man of vision as he aged, the petulant nature of his youth now maturing as he realized how quickly time was passing. His trading post grew in importance and value. Rolling casks of local tobacco could be seen on the docks awaiting transport to England. Farmers brought their crops there to trade for the necessities of life which they couldn't produce on their own farms. A young George Washington even stopped there once while on a surveying mission, declaring the area a place of great natural beauty. Meanwhile with the death of Thomas and his wife Louisa, The Refuge began to fall into disrepair.

Some fifty years later, Greyson was owned by the son of the man who won it from Thomas. From its prominent siting on the tributary of the Potomac River, it was an easy target for British frigates. During the War for American Independence, a British ship fired on Greyson from the river but missed it entirely. Though the shelling did no damage to the house, the beautifully landscaped grounds were ruined. Greyson played its part during the Civil War as well. In 1864, the house was taken over by, first, Confederate and then Union troops and served as headquarters and hospital for the occupying armies. Troops drilled back and forth across what had once been Greyson's magnificent lawns. At war's end, the house and estate, much the worse for wear after two wars and neglect, then transferred to the loving hands of a soldier who had been stationed at Greyson during the war. His family occupied the house and grounds for the next 145 years.

In 1930, the old house, not much altered from the original appearance which Thomas Grey designed, along with the remaining seven hundred acres, was inherited by James Thurman, a retired United States Congressman, who used it as a hunting retreat. The seven hundred acres supported crop production of corn, soybeans, wheat and barley, as well as pasture, woods and marshes. His wife Flora had been raised in poverty and had worked after the Great War as a hostess in a restaurant in DC frequented by members of Congress. There she met James Thurman, with whom she fell in love and married. James had served several terms in Congress, and then decided to retire to his estate in Virginia. Thrilled to have been the wife of a Congressman and having a great love for history, Flora seemed not to recognize that the country was in the grips of the Great Depression and set about to restore the old house to its former grandeur. She and James moved to the house with their son Jimmy and began its renovation.

Flora assembled a team of architects, workmen, landscape architects and structural engineers to bring her vision to life. The original kitchen, a small brick house set behind the main house to prevent the spread of food odors and extreme heat and to reduce the risk of fire, was now turned into a studio for Flora's many projects. Its large fireplace, where once slaves had prepared extravagant meals for the owners, now warmed the worktable and artist easel where Flora created her art projects. The original laundry, a separate brick building near the kitchen, stood near a deep well and was now used as a potting shed. Its shelves were lined with clay pots, potting soil and gardening tools. When the restoration work on the house was nearly completed, Flora's team began developing the site plans and gardens. Soon thereafter, brick walks and walls began to take shape alongside sunken flower beds, grassy alleys and a vast variety of specimen tree plantings along a centered green.

Flora and her workmen created a garden of boxwood hedges and planted crepe myrtle and dogwood trees for shade. On one side Flora's workmen planted an allee of cherry trees that blossomed pink in the spring. On the other side, an evergreen-bordered walk led to a pergola with double swings for relaxing and enjoying the pastoral setting. Other features include another potting shed in the Chippendale style and a workshop and green-house. Roses and camellias of various shades were scattered about the garden for color. Flora was frequently seen in a road coach pulled by two enormous bays as she surveyed the work in progress. All involved agreed that the final outcome was enchanting. The work that she supervised, which led to her husband's ultimate heart attack, firmly established the structure in the minds of Virginians as one of the Old Dominion's noblest estates. It was this house with its seven hundred acres which James and Flora's granddaughter Peyton Thurman inherited from her parents Jimmy and Dorothy.

Three weeks after the somber rain-soaked funeral for her parents, Peyton closed the door of her tiny London flat and walked glumly downstairs. On the street corner, she pulled the tie of her tan Burberry coat tighter around her trim waist and hailed a taxicab for Heathrow Airport. At the airport, Peyton grumbled under her breath at the tight security measures she was forced to undergo. Secretly, though, she felt a sense of relief that the checks were in place. Never a happy flier, Peyton traveled by plane as little as possible. To her great relief, however, her flight over the Atlantic Ocean was unremarkable, except for some turbulence near the States. The in-flight movie was a forgettable chick flick which she slept through. The in-flight meal was some sort of pasta which she pushed around the plastic dish, finally eating only the plastic-wrapped brownie and drinking a cup of coffee.

When the plane's landing gear was released noisily and the plane itself landed with a thud on the runway, Peyton waited for the thrill she usually experienced on returning to her native soil. But oddly, all she felt was a dull...what?...a dull something in the pit of her stomach. She couldn't quite pinpoint the feeling till she walked through the customs gate and began searching the crowd.

Then it was that it hit her. There was no one to meet her. In years past, whenever she'd come home for a visit, her parents had usually driven to Dulles to meet her plane. Dorothy, a short, athletic woman, had usually made some ridiculous cardboard sign to greet her. And Jimmy, her father, had said the same thing every time - "Well, I think so - it's about time you came home!" Then he'd wrapped her in his big bear hug and grabbed her carry-on bag.

Well, no more of that, Peyton, she told herself. *Things are going to be different from now on so you'd just better adjust.*

She squared her shoulders, and headed for the baggage pick-up area. As soon as her bags came through the opening on the carousel, she grabbed them and made her way to the taxi stand. Raising her hand, she hailed a car, and handed a bag to the driver.

Home, she thought.

Chapter Three:

Cameron

As soon as Peyton settled herself into the backseat of the cab for the twenty-minute ride from the airport, she pulled her cellphone from her bag and began making notes.

To Do List

- Open Greyson
- Talk to farm manager about day to day operations on the farm
- Buy plane ticket back to London
- Text farm manager re: plans for the future

Soon the bustling congestion of office buildings and airport support buildings gave way to rolling farmland and livestock grazing on the hillsides. Peyton could practically feel her heart rate slowing. She took deep breaths and looked out the window expectantly. At length she saw the painted wooden sign beside the stone pillars.

"Greyson," the sign read in dark green letters on an ivory background. The farm itself was completely surrounded by a stone wall. The mortarless walls running up and down hills made an imposing sight and Peyton's breath caught at the sight of it. Off in the distance to the west, the Blue Ridge Mountains rose in majestic splendor.

Greyson was never more delightful than in the spring of the year. Visitors to the grand manor house drove on a long gravel drive that passed between two rows of tall hardwoods under-planted with azaleas of every color. Horse pastures bounded the drive on both sides. Around a final bend in the road, the house loomed, an immense red brick Georgian building with tall windows framed in white and a hipped slate roof bearing a dozen dormers. The house backed up to a scenic tributary of the Potomac River. Beside the river, paths covered in pea gravel meandered along the hillside. A colonial kitchen garden and maze as well as a paddock separated the house from the dock further down the sloping hillside at water's edge. In Thomas Grey's time the water side of the house had been the main entrance, so a grand doorway overlooked the river scene. But sometime in the nineteenth century, traffic from the dusty corduroy road outside the property began to be heavier than river traffic. James and Flora decided sometime in the late thirties to add a long covered porch along the rear of the house, a cool place to rest in the evenings in one of the rocking chairs that were always there. So an equally grand portico was constructed for the other side of the house as well. It was to that entrance that the taxi arrived. Peyton looked out the window as if trying to find her bearings.

Surrounding the house on either side were outbuildings of every variety. On the east side were a smokehouse, laundry, dairy and kitchen building. On the west side were a carriage house, five-stall stable and a dovecote.

Greyson was where Peyton had grown up, raised calves for the local 4-H club, and had learned to ride horses. It was home but also, now, quite empty of the people who had made it so.

I didn't realize what we had here until I went away.

Peyton surveyed the property gloomily. A pall hung over her as she emerged from the taxi and paid the driver. *The boxwoods need trimming,* she thought. She rolled her bags up to the steps and carried them onto the wide front porch. Turning the key in the brass box lock of the heavily paneled door, she took a deep breath, stepped inside and looked around.

The front porch opened to a wide center hall with 12-foot ceilings, ornate plaster moldings, transoms and large windows and doors that faced one another for cross-ventilation. Two large rooms opened off each side of the hall. Floors throughout were of wide heart pine boards polished to a high sheen. The ceiling height throughout the house soared to ten feet. The walls of the center hall were deeply paneled in walnut and a staircase six feet in width led to the upper floor. Family portraits painted in oils lined the staircase all the way to the carved arch that surmounted it. Peyton smiled wistfully as she saw the portrait of herself as a three year old with her mother and father and Dusty, her new pony. Dusty had been her daily companion for years until she outgrew him. On the landing at the top of the stairs, a nine and one-half foot tall case clock maintained a steady beat marking the passage of time in the old house. Beneath the steps, a door led to a full basement where, Peyton knew, her parents had stored antiques, junk and memorabilia from their years of residence at Greyson.

It's odd, she thought, how a house can go down when there's no one to live in it. In just the four weeks since her parents' death, the house had taken on a smell Peyton had never noticed before. Her footsteps seemed to echo unbearably loudly as she moved down the halls on the old wooden floorboards. She walked around the house carefully, memories assaulting her at each room's doorway.

The front parlor to the right of the front door was completely paneled in rich heart pine. Arched recesses on either side of the fireplace sheltered the tall windows set into 18 inch thick solid brick walls. Beneath the windows, window seats cushioned in pale blue velvet beckoned invitingly. An oriental carpet in faded blue and rose covered the pine floor. Atop the marble fireplace, a large painting of a group of racehorses rested in a frame of gold leaf. (Her mother Dorothy had commissioned that painting for her father the first year they'd gone to the Derby.) To the left of the front door, a sitting room contained a full length portrait of Louisa Grey which hung above a nearly eight foot long Chippendale sofa upholstered in dusty rose damask. In the center of the room, rococo candlesticks of sterling silver stood at each of the four corners of a mahogany Chippendale gaming table.

Through a carved archway, the dining room to the left of the center hall held a polished mahogany table and twelve chairs under a brass chandelier of ancient age. Family silver held pride of place on the large inlaid mahogany sideboard along one plastered wall. The same window pane where Thomas Grey had carved his and his bride's names over 200 years ago looked out upon a landscape hardly changed from that time until the present. Peyton remembered countless birthday and holiday celebrations around that table and smiled to herself. With a daunting realization that the care of the house now fell to her, she moved on through hallways, kitchen, library, and conservatory.

Peyton peeked in room after room, as though seeking to convince herself that her parents were really gone. She picked up her suitcases and climbed the wooden treads of the staircase, holding carefully to the bannister railing. Finally, after looking briefly into each of the five other bedrooms along the hall, she reached the room on the second floor where she'd always slept. This had been her room from birth until she left for college at age 18. After that she'd only lived there during summers and holidays. Still, it felt more like home than her London flat.

Looking around, she tossed her bags onto the carpet and sighed audibly. She threw herself onto the blue toile de Jouy fabric covering one of the twin mahogany rice canopy beds and wiped away a tear. Above the beds were canopies of cotton fishnet woven in intricate designs. The room looked the same as when she had last visited three weeks before. Same heavy cornflower blue draperies at the two windows, same mantel and fireplace, same closet and dressing room. The bathroom was still there and so were her old dolls. But the house was so empty without her parents. She closed her eyes and sighed again. Fatigue from hours of travel and packing soon overtook her and she fell into a deep sleep.

It was not until an hour and a half later that the insistent ringing of the telephone beside her bed woke her. She shook her head to clear the cobwebs and sat up.

"Hello," Peyton responded somewhat grumpily.

"Peyton? It's Cam...Cameron Hill. Have you got a minute to talk?"

Cameron, Peyton thought. *Oh, yes, the farm foreman, of course,* and she shook her head as though to clear the cobwebs.

"Peyton, I know you've just gotten in but I wonder if we could meet sometime. We need to talk about what's next."

"Oh, yes, of course, you'd need to know what to do now since..."

"If this is a bad time," Cameron suggested," maybe tomorrow would be easier. I know you must be tired from travelling."

"No, we might as well tackle this now as later. Can you come up to the house in about thirty minutes?"

"That'll be fine. See you then," Cameron said quietly and hung up the phone.

Peyton spent the next few minutes brushing the knots out of her long, dark brown hair, and pulled it back into a high pony tail. She washed the sleep from her eyes and changed to a fresh pair of khakis and a white cotton sweater, then walked downstairs. She grabbed a small glass bottle of Coke from the refrigerator in the kitchen and smiled. Her daddy always had to have his Cokes and they never tasted better than when they were in the glass bottles. Walking through the heavy screen door to the back porch, Peyton sat in one of the eight large rockers there. The vista from the back porch had always been inspiring. This afternoon she found it downright comforting, as though it was one of the few things in her life that hadn't changed. Hummingbirds flitted about Dorothy's feeder. Jimmy's horses grazed quietly in the pasture beyond. *Only Mama and Daddy are missing*, she thought. Soon she heard the sound of tires on gravel and got up to meet Greyson's farm manager.

Peyton walked toward the end of the porch and saw a tall, lanky and rather dirty man emerge from a dusty blue pick-up and step carefully onto the porch floor. His brown hair was cropped close and his eyes were almost shockingly blue. The skin on his arms was tanned and firm and he looked as though there could be no job too difficult for him to perform. Their eyes met and almost immediately, Cameron Hill removed his cap from his head, folded it and tucked it in his back pocket.

"Forgive me if we don't shake hands. I just got in from the barn and I'm kinda dusty."

"Never mind, Cameron," Peyton replied and shook his hand anyway. "How've you been?"

"Okay, trying to stay ahead of the weeds and the bugs, ya know," he grinned. "I thought you'd want to talk about what you're going to do with Greyson."

"Sure, Cameron, have a seat. I'm just enjoying the view. Can I get you something to drink?."

"Just some water."

Peyton got up immediately, went to the kitchen and ran some water into a heavy glass. Then she plopped a couple of ice cubes from the freezer into the glass, and walked back out to the porch. Cameron stood as she came up to him.

"Here ya go."

"Thanks."

Cameron eased his tall frame into the rocker next to Peyton and swatted a fly from his head. They made small talk about her flight and the weather.

Peyton noticed how easy he was to talk to. He proceeded to tell her every-thing that went on at Greyson. The foreman managed an almost Jeffersonian approach to farming and did it all with a small staff of workers. Peyton knew that her father had raised Black Angus cattle on the property as well as a small selection of fine Thoroughbred horses. The cattle and horses were bred, raised and sold at auction each year. In addition, corn, wheat, soybeans, and alfalfa were grown in the fields of Greyson surrounding the manor house. Vegetables and herbs were cultivated in a kitchen garden down a slope from the main house and a greenhouse nestled young plants, shrubs and trees before they were ready to be transplanted to the grounds. A water garden with a Koi pond with flowing stream featured a Chinese Chippendale arched bridge painted a glossy bright red. Over the course of their thirty-year tenancy, Peyton's mother and father had continued to return the estate to magnificence. Cameron, along with a group of dedicated farm hands, had run the farm for over ten years with the wholehearted support of Peyton's parents who often spoke of him as if he were their son.

Cameron returned their affection by maintaining the property as though it were his very own. He constantly checked the water lines, the heating systems, the pastures, the livestock, and the crops. Jimmy and Dorothy had found Cameron to be indispensable to the success of their operation, espe-cially as they grew older.

"So, anyway," he continued, "I was wondering if you'd decided what the future of Greyson was going to be. Have you thought about whether you'll be keeping it or selling it? If you keep it, will you be living here or return to England and rent the place out? I know it may be too soon for you to know yet, but you at least need to start thinking about your plans."

Peyton closed her eyes and ran a hand across her face in a gesture of tiredness. She opened her eyes and looked far out across the fields and pas-ture, past the hardwood forest that surrounded the cultivated land and even farther to the rolling mountains that rose in the distance. *How am I supposed to answer him when I don't have a clue what to do?*

Up until now, her life had been pretty simple. Peyton had lived alone in London in a small apartment. Her career at the publishing house had been her only concern and she was on the fast track to upper management. . There had been occasional boyfriends but never anyone serious. There just wasn't time. And with any difficult decisions, she'd flown back home to talk over her problems with her parents. Only now, with perhaps the toughest decision of her life to make, there was no one to talk to, no one at all.

She shook her head at the enormity of it all. It just wasn't possible that she could be facing this. What to do?

"Cam, I really don't know just yet. I haven't had time to process all of this."

"I tell you what, Peyton. Why don't you sleep on it tonight? I could pick you up tomorrow morning and we'll have a look around the place. Just to give you a little more information to work from."

"That sounds like a good idea," Peyton responded, rising from her chair. "How does eight o'clock sound?"

"Suits me fine. I'll be here," Cameron said and pulled his cap from his pocket. He fitted it carefully on his head and stepped off the porch. Peyton watched his retreating figure and shook her head again.

Presently, she heard the sound of the engine in Cameron's truck starting up and the crunch of the gravel as the tires took the truck down the lane to the road. Soon all was still and quiet again. Peyton was all alone.

"What am I going to do?" she said out loud to no one and sat back down in the rocker.

Chapter Four:

Alone

THE MORNING LOOMED BRIGHT AND SUNNY OUTSIDE THE LONG windows in Peyton's bedroom, yet she sat at her dressing table staring gloomily into her reflection in the mirror. She shook her head to clear her vision, but still everything seemed out of focus. She checked the time on her cellphone and looked again into the mirror.

Now what was I supposed to do this morning, she pondered. *Oh yes, Cameron's coming over for a drive. I better have a shower and a bite to eat.*

She took a quick shower in the white tiled bathroom that adjoined her bedroom, then wrapped herself in a thick towel and walked over to her closet. Selecting a pair of jeans and a white tee shirt from the dresser drawer, she dressed hurriedly and slipped on a pair of Chuck Taylors. She grabbed up her hairbrush and pulled it through her thick brown tresses before descending the winding staircase to the entry hall.

In the kitchen, she found a bowl and spoon and mixed up some instant grits to warm in the microwave while the smell of freshly brewed coffee permeated the kitchen. She got a can of frozen orange juice concentrate from the freezer and plopped it into her mother's cut glass pitcher. Selecting a wooden spoon from the drawer, she added water and stirred the mixture until its bright orange color looked and felt right. After pouring her orange juice into an old fashioned glass, she set it on a lacquered tray and pulled a white linen napkin and silver spoon from the sideboard drawer in the dining room. Taking the bowl of grits from the microwave, she spread a pat of butter on top and put it beside the napkin. She set her tray down upon the highly polished mahogany of the dining table and raised the spoon to her lips when a sharp rap was heard on the back door.

Of course it was Cameron and she invited him in. She offered him a bowl of grits which he refused saying he'd eaten an hour ago. She moved briskly to the coffeemaker and poured him a cup. Then they sat at the dining table while Peyton finished her breakfast. Conversation was superficial and the meal was hurried. After finishing her grits, Peyton poured a cup of black coffee into a travel mug, made another one for Cameron, and set the dirty dishes in the sink.

"I'll deal with those later," she said.

Grabbing her backpack, Peyton slung a cap on her head and walked by Cameron's side to his truck parked in the drive behind the house.

"So what if I decide to sell the place," Peyton said sliding into the passenger side. "What happens to you?"

"Boy, you get right to the heart of the matter, don't you?" Cameron answered.

"Look, I'm in the publishing business. There's never a lot of time for small talk. We live and die around deadlines, so I guess I'm not in the habit of beating around the bush. I haven't lived here for several years, just came back for visits as you know, so things must have changed a lot. I figure you're the farm expert here. I need your advice."

"To be blunt, if you sell, you make a pile of money." Cameron said, clearing his throat, "I suppose I'll have to look for something else to do, someplace else to go."

An uncomfortable silence hung in the air between them for a moment. Peyton ran her fingers along the edge of the seat and encountered a child's stuffed toy - a rabbit, a whimsical yellow plaything that seemed to have little in common with the silent Cameron Hill.

She pulled it out from under the seat, smiled, and showed it to him.

"This yours?" she asked.

"It belongs to my daughter," he answered and retrieved it from her. He placed the animal in the glove compartment of the truck, and then turned down a dusty lane that divided two fields of corn.

"Here's where I thought we'd start this morning, Peyton. This is where your dad and I were working last. I thought you'd like to see exactly what goes on in running this place since you've been gone so long"

For the rest of the day, Peyton and Cameron drove from field to pasture, examining machinery, looking at the status of livestock and crops, peering into dusty barns and stables, checking belts and harness, and inspecting the storage shelters for feed, seed, chemicals, and fertilizers. They stopped only once at noon for lunch. The two of them drove ten miles up the highway to a tiny country store at a crossroads intersection. There, sitting on the tailgate of Cameron's truck, they made a meal out of packs of crackers, cans of Vienna sausages, and bottles of Coke.

"Not exactly fine dining like you're used to in London, is it?"

"No, but I kinda like it. Reminds me of hanging out with my daddy when I was a kid."

"Well, we better roll if we want to see any more."

"Let's do it," Peyton responded, surprised to see how much she was enjoying herself.

It was a day that Peyton had dreaded at its beginning because she knew it would show the big empty space that her parents' passing had created. She'd lost so much with the death of her parents. Yet by day's end, though she felt exhausted, somehow she was exhilarated by the sheer energy and diversification of her parents' operation. Her parents had been remarkable stewards of their land for decades. Cameron and Peyton planned to go out again the next day to finish exploring the farm. Peyton was to drive over to Cameron's house at seven o'clock the next morning to start the tour. It was only when Cameron returned her to the house and Peyton was left alone that gloom settled over her once again.

Four miles away in his small house up a dirt road, Cameron Hill tucked his two-year-old daughter into her wooden crib for the night. He ran his fingers along her sleeper-clad arm and smiled. He handed her the tiny rabbit he'd brought in from the truck and placed it carefully next to her. Leaning down, he kissed her smooth forehead and smelled the sweet smell of her blond hair.

We're alone, he thought, and shook his head sadly.

Chapter Five:

Breakfast with Ruthie

AT THE FIRST LIGHT OF MORNING, CAMERON BEGAN STIR-
ring. He heard the soft coos of Ruthie in the next room, talking to her little
rabbit. A smile crossed Cameron's face and he turned to face the empty
pillow beside him.

Gone! It never ceased to surprise him how sharp was the pain he felt.
His wife Jane had been dead a year now, cut down at age 33 by a particularly
virulent strain of cancer that had hardly given him time to prepare himself for
life without her. There was even less time to think of being a single parent.

He and Jane had been married for almost ten years before she'd con-
ceived. For years they'd been told Jane couldn't have children so her preg-
nancy came as a surprise. They'd gone through it together - Jane teasing
him about his sympathetic nausea when she had morning sickness, Cameron
going with Jane to Lamaze classes and into the delivery room with her.

For nearly a year their happiness was complete. Ruthie was a perfect
baby and Jane breastfed her with no difficulty. Then when Ruthie was about
nine months old, Jane began having occasional headaches and dizzy spells.
She attributed them to being tired from caring for the baby and tried to ignore
them. Soon, though she began vomiting after every meal and her doctor
diagnosed a brain tumor. Only a few months later, Jane was dead.

Cameron had planned a small funeral service for her which was attended by the friends they'd had in the community. After the funeral, there was a brief graveside ceremony in the small churchyard of the tiny Methodist church a few miles up the road from his house. Cameron and Ruthie went there occasionally to put a bouquet of fresh flowers against the tombstone.

The first few visits had been difficult and he'd ended up wiping away tears the entire time he was there. But during the past few months, he and Ruthie had been happier and the trip was easier.

Now, though, there was the chance that another big change would enter their lives. What if Peyton decided to sell the farm? Where would he go? What would he do? And what about Ruthie? After a difficult adjustment, she'd finally become accustomed to the day care center she attended each day while Cameron worked. He didn't know what he'd do if he had to make another change in her young life now.

Well, all the moaning in the world wouldn't make a difference so he'd just have to get up and face the day. Throwing the covers back, Cameron stood and wiped the sleep from his eyes. Checking first to make sure Ruthie was still playing contentedly, he walked briskly to the bathroom, dropped his boxers and turned on the shower, the sound of the water drowning out the questions in his head.

A few moments later, he emerged from the shower dripping rivulets of water onto the bath mat. He toweled off and slipped on a fresh pair of boxers, then went back into his room.

Pulling on the jeans he'd worn yesterday, he walked barefoot into Ruthie's room. She was standing in her crib, her arms outstretched to Cameron. He smiled and said, "There's my girl," and grabbed her up and out of the crib.

A quick diaper change and a warm wet washcloth on her face and Ruthie was ready to be dressed. Already full of opinions about her wardrobe,

Ruthie pulled her father by the hand over to her closet. Cameron brought down two shirts, a blue flowered print and a solid yellow shirt with a big daisy appliquéd in front. Ruthie, of course, selected the yellow shirt as Cameron knew she would. Yellow was Ruthie's current favorite color and she always chose clothes in that shade. Cameron dressed her in a pair of jeans with an elastic waist and shoes and socks, and Ruthie ran toward the kitchen.

Cameron grabbed a khaki long sleeved shirt from the closet and pulled it on as he chased Ruthie through the house. He rolled up the sleeves to his elbow and was just about to button the shirt when he heard a sharp knock at the front door.

Picking up Ruthie and holding her at his side like a football, Cameron skidded to the front door with Ruthie's giggles as background music. He opened the door and looked into Peyton's eyes.

"Mornin'," she said, her eyes opening a little wider as she glimpsed the triangle of dark hair across Cameron's chest. "Am I too early?"

"Oh, shoot, I guess I slept in a little. Rain on the roof always does that to me. What time is it?" Cameron said, feeling for the wristwatch that was still on his nightstand.

"It's 7:00 just like you said. What's for breakfast?"

"Ummm, that may be a bit of a problem, unless you like Count Chocula and coffee."

"Sounds perfect. Sign me up," said Peyton reaching her forefinger to tickle Ruthie's middle. "Who's this?"

"This is my daughter, Ruthie," Cameron said with a smile. "She's two."

"She looks like you around the eyes. I bet she keeps you busy.

After an awkward pause, Peyton continued, "Mama and Daddy told me about Jane. I'm so sorry. How have you managed on your own?"

"Well, some days, just barely. Seems like I can never keep up with the laundry and housekeeping. But the farm work around here keeps me sane. And Ruthie gives me something to live for," he smiled ruefully, looking down at the small child with affection. "She stays with a lady in town who's great with her."

Ruthie wriggled out of Cameron's arms and ran to the kitchen ahead of Cameron. Pulling her high chair away from the wall, she reached her little foot up to the step to try to get in. Buttoning his shirt and tucking it into his jeans, Cameron followed the toddler into the kitchen.

"Whoa, hoss," Cameron said, with a chuckle," You better wait for some help," and scooped her up into the seat. "Now about that breakfast…"

Peyton sat at the table and talked to Ruthie while Cameron got out bowls and spoons from the cabinets. The smell of fresh coffee soon filled the small kitchen and the trio sat down to three bowls filled with Count Chocula, the only cereal Ruthie would eat.

"Whatdya think of our high class cuisine?" Cameron said with a smile.

"Hey, I never complain if I don't have to fix it."

"We used to eat breakfast at your mama's table occasionally. It was sure better than this. You know, I thought a lot of your parents. They always treated me like a son," Cameron said thoughtfully.

"Thanks, Cameron," Peyton said quietly. "That means a lot. I miss them…so much. You know, we're both pretty much alone now. But at least you still have Ruthie."

"Yeah, I'm lucky to have her. But I'm happy to loan her to you – diaper changing times she's always available."

"Remind me to get back to you on that," Peyton said with a smile, scooping up the last of her cereal. "Now, let's hit the road. We still have a lot of ground to cover."

Putting the dishes in the sink, Cameron lifted Ruthie from her high chair, stuck a finger in her diaper, and smiled.

"Still dry!"

He collected her diaper bag, picked up Ruthie and pointed Peyton toward the back door.

"Let's go," he said.

After buckling Ruthie in the car seat in the back seat of the truck's cab, Cameron settled himself in the driver's seat and watched as Peyton strapped herself in. For a split second, he flashed back to the hundreds of times he'd watched Jane do the same thing. Then, catching himself, he whistled a little tune and started up the engine.

The road in front of Cameron's house was quiet and contained few houses. Fields of green were interspersed with patches of woods. The three watched as field and forest zipped by. Cameron pulled the truck over to the roadside every couple of miles to look at a field of corn or soybeans, a pasture full of cattle, or a storage shed of some kind. Occasionally, Ruthie would sing a little song and smile at the two adults.

It's amazing, Peyton thought. *These two have lost so much, yet they still seem so happy. I wonder if I'll ever get there.*

Pulling the truck to a stop beside a pasture, Cameron stilled the engine, unbuckled Ruthie and said, "Let's take a look at this."

Peyton unbuckled her seatbelt and opened the door. Without looking, she hopped out of the truck. Her foot immediately slipped out from under her on a patch of wet grass and she slid down into the ditch.

"Oh crap!" she said.

"Cwap," Ruthie mocked her and Peyton winced from her mistake.

"Sorry, Cameron. I've gotta be more careful in what I say. I forgot how little kids are."

"Don't worry about it" Cameron said, carrying Ruthie around to Peyton's side of the truck. "You o.k.? With the rain last night, I guess the grass is still kinda slick." He tried hard but unsuccessfully to hide the smile that grew on his face. Peyton's jeans were covered in mud. "Good Lord, when you fall, you really do it up right!"

He reached his free hand down to grab Peyton's and pulled her upright but her foot slipped again. She grabbed for Cameron with her other hand to right herself but pulled Cameron and Ruthie down into the muddy ditch with her.

All three of them looked at each other in stunned silence for a second and then burst out laughing. Ruthie grabbed handfuls of mud in tiny dimpled hands and tossed them at the two adults. A splatter of mud hit Peyton right on her cheek and, in surprise, she grabbed Ruthie with a tickle who picked up a handful of mud and placed it on top of her father's cap where it promptly ran down his hair.

Laughing loudly, the three mud-covered ditch dwellers began tossing mud blobs back and forth until eventually all three were covered from head to toe with mud. A lone car passed by on the road and slowed as the driver looked quizzically at the three in the ditch, then drove on.

"Well, it'll be all over town now. That was Miss Lettie. She's the worst gossip in the county," Cameron acknowledged. "We better get cleaned up. Lord, Peyton, you look awful."

"Oh and you look so good by comparison?"

"Daddy funny," Ruthie laughed and grabbed his cheeks. Planting a muddy kiss right on Cameron's lips, she said, "Again, Daddy."

"No, I think we've had enough mud for today. We better go wash off. Come on, Peyton, there's a water trough up this path."

One hundred feet up the path that ran alongside the field, an old footed bathtub stood beside a pipe with a short length of hose attached.

"This is where I water the cattle when they're in this field. Here ya go - ladies first," he said, handing the hose to Peyton.

Peyton hosed Ruthie down and then sprayed herself until most of the mud was gone and her hair was plastered to her head. Her wet tee shirt clung embarrassingly to her breasts and she pulled it away, and then tossed the hose to Cameron sending the spray into his face. Ruthie scrunched up her nose, then looked at her dad and laughed.

"Daddy wet!" she cried.

The hose, meanwhile, which had dropped to the ground, was writhing about, making it difficult to pick up. Finally, Cameron grabbed the nozzle and began hosing himself off. He unbuttoned his shirt and took it off, holding it at arm's length to rinse. Occasionally, he trained the hose directly on Peyton, causing her to shriek with laughter.

"Hey, I was just helpin' you out – there was a spot you missed," he said without cracking a smile.

Finally the three got most of the mud from their clothes and sat in the pasture to dry off a bit. Ruthie pulled handfuls of grass and tickled her father's nose. Cameron stretched out in the soft grass and clasped his hands behind his head. Peyton reached out to run her fingers through Ruthie's fine golden hair and looked admiringly at the man beside her.

Good grief, even wet and dirty, he's gorgeous, she thought to herself. *Why haven't I ever noticed that before?*

After a while, Cameron looked apologetically at Peyton and said, "Well, I guess we won't get to see much of the farm today. I'm sorry about that. Now that we're not so wet, maybe we should go back home and get cleaned up."

"Hey, I need to be the one apologizing. I was the one who fell in the mud in the first place. You wanna try again tomorrow? I do need to go back to the house and take a shower."

"Yeah, that's a good idea. I need to get Ruthie out of this wet stuff. C'mon, let's go back to the truck."

The three still-damp riders got into the truck and settled themselves for the ride back to Greyson to drop off Peyton. They'd decided to leave Peyton's car at Cameron's house until she could get cleaned up. Soon Ruthie fell asleep in her car seat. It was an uncharacteristically quiet ride with Peyton stealing shy glances at the man who drove the truck.

I must look horrible, she thought.

Cameron rolled the window down and let the sun and fresh air dry his hair. His shirt had been tossed in the truck bed along with his cap. His brown arms stretched out along the seat back and on the window ledge. Finally, the truck made its way up the long drive to Greyson and rolled to a stop near the back porch. He turned the key off in the ignition and sat quietly for a minute, then turned to see that Ruthie was still asleep.

Cameron chuckled as he took a long look at Peyton, shook his head and said, "I can't say I've ever had a morning like this before. It was... interesting."

"Yeah, actually, it was kinda fun," Peyton replied, stroking Ruthie's curls. "I say we do it again."

"OK but without the mud. I'm not much good at laundry."

"Can you come by later this afternoon so I can pick up my car?"

"Sounds good. I've got to pick up some fertilizer in town. You can ride with me if you want to."

With that, Peyton emerged from the truck and walked up the tall steps to her house. "Her house." That's what it was beginning to feel like now.

I wonder: Can I sell it? Should I? She thought, then turned at the top step to wave to Cameron below as the pickup truck's engine growled to a start.

He backed it up and turned the truck around. It kicked up the round gravel of the driveway as it made its way away from Greyson.

Peyton watched the glow of the taillights as the truck braked to a stop at the highway; a little sadness settled over her again as the emptiness of her house surrounded her.

Unlocking the back door, she slipped off her shoes by the door, and closed the door. Then she padded up the stairs and headed to her bedroom.

Oh yes, another shower was going to feel really good!

Chapter Six:

A Visit to the Barn

THREE DAYS LATER PEYTON EMERGED FROM THE BACK DOOR of the house and stood for a moment on the porch to look around. A slight breeze stirred the hammock at the porch's end. The rocking chairs, painted in thick coats of greenish-black paint, looked out upon a scene of morning majesty. As always, Peyton was amazed at the simple beauty of the land surrounding Greyson. In the yard near the flagstone patio, the old iron bell still stood atop a tall cedar post. Near the house were the many outbuildings of the original estate that had belonged to Thomas Grey - the laundry, kitchen, two storehouses, all with pedimented roofs and a round brick dovecote near a line of Lombardy poplars. Beyond these, the surrounding fields were fenced, some to contain the hundreds of Black Angus cattle or Thoroughbred horses that grazed quietly and some to enclose fields of corn or beans. Peyton skipped down the steps, breathing in the fresh morning air as she went. She'd been back home barely a week and, after seeing the farm with Cameron earlier, had decided to drive around the property alone this morning. Walking briskly, she settled a ball cap over her ponytail and headed for the carriage house where she knew her father had kept the small golf cart he used for driving around his farm.

At the carriage house, she unlocked the padlock and slid the door to the side. The cart, ivory in color with the name Greyson painted in dark green lettering on the hood sat in the dark building. Peyton climbed in. Turning the key, she started the cart instantly and backed it out of the building.

"Bless Daddy," she thought. *"He always kept everything in such perfect order."*

Peyton maneuvered the cart down dusty lanes, through fields of knee-high corn and soybeans, and finally back to the fenced pastures. In one of these pastures, cattle moved slowly and stopped to graze. In another, Thoroughbred colts and fillies kicked up their heels and chased each other while their mares watched nearby. In two smaller fenced pastures farther away from the main house, a mahogany bay stallion and an Angus bull grazed quietly, occasionally picking up their heads as if to sniff the air.

Peyton drove the cart finally to the big white barn nearest the pasture where the horses were grazing. She noticed that Cameron's dusty blue pickup was parked just outside the main doorway and slid her golf cart alongside it. She felt an unaccustomed feeling of gladness at the prospect of seeing him. Jumping out, she walked quickly up the inclined path to the doorway and peered in.

The building itself, a typical English barn structure, was painted white outside with a green slate roof. The walls were sixteen feet in height and stretched nearly 100 feet in length. Constructed of huge beams of oak, the barn was nearly a hundred years old. It had seen decades of crops and held hundreds of bags of feed and fertilizer within its walls.

Waiting a moment for her eyes to adjust to the darkness inside after the bright sun outside, Peyton stepped onto the tongue-and-groove oak flooring of the barn and felt her heart skip a beat as she saw Cameron with Ruthie at his feet. Stepping into the dim light of the barn, she called out to him.

"Good morning! I just thought I'd have a look around the barn," she said.

Cameron turned at the sound of her voice, smiled in spite of himself and called a greeting.

The three walked around the cool, dark interior of the huge building, talking quietly. Cameron pointed out the tack room and a small office where he worked occasionally. The office held an old wooden desk and office chair, a metal file cabinet and, atop the desk, a laptop. An old leather stirrup rested on a stack of papers. A small window unit air conditioner cooled the room.

Back out in the barn, Ruthie scampered around the stalls picking up bits of hay and sticks to show her father. Seeing the tenderness with which Cameron addressed his daughter brought a small stab of pain to Peyton's heart.

Life is not fair, she thought. *This innocent little child is without her mother, Cameron is without his wife, and I'm without my parents. Life is just not fair.*

But those thoughts quickly left her as she looked at the joy on Cameron's face as he picked up Ruthie and swung her around. The toddler giggled with delight and said, "Again, Daddy." So of course, he did it again. Then he carefully set his daughter down and sent her to pick up her stuffed rabbit which had fallen in the swinging.

"You know, there's something we really should talk about," Cameron said hesitantly. "I'm not sure if you know this or not but there's a lien on this property. Your daddy got it refinanced just before the plane crash. He had inherited from his great uncle a few acres and an old house up the road from the far end of the property. It used to be a part of the original Greyson property a hundred years ago. Your daddy was talking about fixing up the old house and planting more trees. Maybe you better go down to the bank and talk to Taylor, see what you can do."

"Is Taylor Jamison still running the bank in town? I thought he'd be retired by now. He and my parents used to be in the same bridge club until his divorce."

"Not only is he running it, but he's been working with a big-time wheeler dealer from Chicago to develop some of the farmland around here. He was talking to your daddy about buying up some of his land. You know –I think he wants to put up more McMansions – just what we need," Cameron added sarcastically.

"I guess I do need to go see him and refinance to put the loan in my name, but I'm not sure about selling him any of my land for development. Why don't you and Ruthie come into town and get some lunch with me? Maybe I'll stop in and make an appointment at the bank to talk to Taylor while we're there."

"Sounds good. I know just where we oughta go. C'mon squirt, let's go for a ride," Cameron called and Ruthie ran toward him gleefully.

Peyton left her cart parked outside the barn and rode with Cameron and Ruthie to the small town of Braverton Mill. Cameron looked over at her and smiled.

"You're in for a culinary delight," he said!

Chapter Seven:

The Schoolhouse Cafe

THE LITTLE TOWN OF BRAVERTON MILL SEEMED AN ANACH-
ronism. No wider than five streets, the town had been settled in the decade
before the Civil War. Nestled on the banks of a tributary of the Potomac River
to the east, a rail line which ran up through Pennsylvania bounded the town
to the west. It was the proximity of the railroad that encouraged the growth
of what originally was a crossroads with one general store. With the arrival
of a train depot in 1853, Braverton Mill had added a one-room schoolhouse
of white clapboard, a tiny stone church and enough houses to fill the five
streets which ran parallel to each other. In the century and a half since then,
the town had maintained a steady population of approximately 300 souls and
never grew much beyond that number. The town existed to serve the farmers
and horse and cattle breeders in the surrounding area.

When the interstate highway system bypassed the town in the 1950s,
Braverton Mill's size was sealed for good, much to the relief of most of its
inhabitants. Now the main street of the town, optimistically named Enterprise
Street, held about twenty shops and businesses, including the original general
store, which had been converted to the County Feeds store, the stone church, a
small café housed in the old schoolhouse, two ladies' apparel shops, five antique
shops, a small grocery, a Shell service station/fast food market, and a John
Deere dealership. Sited at the edge of town was the newly constructed Bank of

Braverton Mill, a square, one-story brick building whose modern façade seemed out of place with the 19th century character of the rest of the town.

Cameron eased his blue pickup into a spot in front of the Schoolhouse Café and looked back at his daughter. Ruthie began kicking her feet against the seat, eager to be released from her car seat. Cameron shook his head and turned his attention to Peyton.

"I'm glad you asked us to come with you," he told her. "It's been nice showing you around the farm these last couple of days. Now, Doodlebug," he said, reaching back and pinching Ruthie's nose, "let's get you some lunch."

He climbed down from the truck, unfastened and picked up Ruthie who had been fidgeting in her car seat behind the two adults. The window by the café's front door bore a sign stating "Come In – We're Open." A sign on the other side of the door proclaimed "Open for breakfast, lunch, dinner and take outs." Peyton followed Cameron and Ruthie into the café and slid into a booth beneath a window.

The large room, once the town's only school, was paneled in pine that had been painted a cream color years ago. A large bulletin board between two of the windows held business cards, lost and found notices and pictures of the town's inhabitants from days gone by.

Behind a counter along one wall, Chub Cole, the short order cook who'd owned the place for the last twenty years was hard at work preparing meals for the dozen or so people who sat around the room. Pulling open the stainless steel door of the refrigerator, he took out hamburger patties, peeled off the paper backing and slapped them on the grill, accompanied by a loud sizzle. He flattened the burgers with his spatula, and then went to work on a basket of French fries deep frying in hot oil nearby. Adjusting the white cap on his head, Chub poured milk into a stainless steel cup and fitted it under the green mixer. Soon, after a whir of the blades, he poured its thick creamy contents into a tall glass and stuck a straw and long handled spoon inside. Flipping the burgers with his spatula and shaking out the basket of fries, he called to the waitress, "Order up!"

At the far end of the building, the day's "Lunch Menu" was written in yellow chalk on a long blackboard, where once children wrote arithmetic problems and spelling words.

Entrees

- Hamburgers
- Cheeseburgers
- Chicken salad plate
- Country ham biscuits
- Fried Chicken
- Barbecue – sandwiches or plates

Sides

- Cole slaw
- French fries
- Mashed potatoes and gravy
- Turnip greens
- Boiled potatoes

Desserts

- Coconut cream pie
- Pecan pie
- Chocolate layer cake

Drinks

- Fresh squeezed lemonade
- Bottled water or Iced tea
- Sodas
- Milk

By 7 PM, most of the food listed on the chalkboard would be gone, sold to the café's loyal following.

Scattered around the single room were five square tables and six booths, three on each side. The placemats were of thin paper with a map of Virginia printed on them. Each map had stars to point out the location of Civil War battles fought in the state.

"Wow, this place never changes," Peyton said with a smile.

"Oh, yes, it does. We're open for breakfast and supper now," said the seventyish woman who brought over two plastic-clad menus, a sheet of paper and a handful of crayons for Ruthie. "Hey, Shug. How're you doin'? I was so sorry to hear about your parents."

"Oh hey, Miss Emmaline," Peyton said, half rising from her seat to give a hug. "Thanks. It's been rough, I'll tell you. Cameron here is helping me sort things out."

"Don't you worry about things if Cameron is taking care of you. You're in good shape. I'll be back in a minute to take your orders."

"I've been coming here since I was Ruthie's age and Emmaline Barker doesn't look like she's aged a day in all that time."

"Yeah, she's one of the best," Cameron agreed. "After Jane died, she brought me meals for about ten nights straight. She's been working here at the Schoolhouse for at least forty years."

"Yeah, I know. I was a year ahead of her granddaughter at Braverton Mill High. We used to come in here after school for shakes and fries all the time. Speaking of that, I'm getting hungry. Are the shakes still as good?"

"Just ask Miss Emmaline. She'll tell you," Cameron said winking to the older lady as she returned.

Pulling her notepad out of her apron pocket, Miss Emmaline said, "Now what'll it be?"

"Cheese," said Ruthie," and Emmaline nodded.

"Sure hon, I'll make you a grilled cheese sandwich. You want some milk?"

Ruthie nodded and set to work coloring her paper.

"I'll have the barbecue plate with slaw and fries and a Coke," said Cameron.

"I'll take the country ham biscuits with boiled potatoes and turnip greens and a glass of sweet tea," Peyton said with a smile.

"I like a girl with a good appetite," Emmaline said as she headed toward Chub with the order.

Ruthie's tongue licked her upper lip as she colored her picture determinedly. Moments later, she held it up to Cameron to admire. He praised it and, turning to Peyton, whispered, "What is it?"

"Mama used to tell me when I'd draw something she didn't recognize, she'd say, 'Tell me about your picture, honey.' That was the safe way out."

"Good idea. I'll remember that from now on."

A quiet fell over the table as Ruthie went back to her picture. The two adults looked around the room expectantly. Cameron stroked Ruthie's hair as she selected another crayon for her drawing.

"You know," Peyton said quietly, "I don't know if I could have handled all this without you. I just didn't realize everything that went on here at Greyson. Even though I grew up there, I didn't pay much attention to the workings of the farm. You've really been a good friend and helped me a lot."

"Well, Ruthie and I have enjoyed hanging out with you, too…except maybe for the mud part," he chuckled. Cameron's eyes twinkled and dimples cut his cheeks in the most delightful way. Peyton's heart did a little flip flop as she looked at him.

Soon Miss Emmaline brought a large oval aluminum tray loaded with their lunch. She began to pass the items around while Cameron tucked a paper napkin into Ruthie's collar. Looking around the table with a self-satisfied air, the older woman beamed at Cameron.

"Now ya'll just holler if you need anything, hear? And don't let me catch you leaving anything on your plates. No diets around here."

Cameron and Peyton looked at each other and grinned. Without another word, they began to dig in to the feast before them.

Chapter Eight:

The Refuge

CAMERON PATTED HIS STOMACH WITH AN EXAGGERATED SIGH of satisfaction.

"Boy, that was good but maybe just one more little bite," he said, wiping the last remnants of barbecue from his lips and stabbing the last boiled potato from Peyton's plate.

"Hey, I was saving that!"

"Too late!" he answered, swallowing the potato, and tickled Ruthie beside him in the booth. "Come on, let's pay up. I got something to show you."

Cameron walked to the cash register and paid while Peyton wiped the last bits of cheese from Ruthie's mouth. Ruthie squirmed in the process but gave Peyton a smile afterward that melted her heart. Holding Ruthie's tiny hand in hers, Peyton walked beside Cameron to the truck.

"I'm paying next time," she said to Cameron. "I insist."

"OK, but we'll be going someplace very expensive then!"

Cameron buckled Ruthie in her car seat while Peyton settled herself in the front seat. He put the truck in gear, backed out of his parking space and headed the truck in the direction of Greyson. He pointed out local landmarks to Ruthie and Peyton, and then pulled into a short gravel driveway by a sign which read, "Little Red Schoolhouse." The cottage at the end of the driveway was an 18th century stone Quaker farmhouse with a larger brick Victorian addition. Behind the house was a large fenced yard containing all sorts of playground equipment. Tall hardwood trees supplied the yard with ample shade.

"This is the lady who keeps Ruthie for me. I'm gonna drop her off for a bit."

Peyton unbuckled Ruthie who crawled into Cameron's waiting arms. The three of them then headed to the farmhouse. There, a grey-haired African-American woman of indeterminate age stood up and reached for Ruthie with a smile.

"Hey, here. I thought you were keeping Ruthie today," the woman said. "How do. I'm Sarah Brown, owner of the Little Red Schoolhouse. My husband Walter carries the mail 'round here."

"Pleased to meet you. I'm Peyton Thurman. I live up at Greyson." She shook Miss Sarah's hand with a firm grip.

"Oh, Law, You're Jimmy and Dorothy's daughter. Your mama and I were co-presidents one year in the garden club. I thought the world of her. I haven't seen you since you were not much older than Ruthie here. I'm so sorry for you I don't know what to do."

"Thank you, Miss Sarah. Cameron is helping me figure out what to do with everything."

"Yeah, that's why I need you to keep Ruthie for an hour or two today, Miss Sarah. Would that be all right?" Cameron asked.

"Why sure, Honey, you all go on outa here. Me and Ruthie gotta check out some new baby chicks Walter just brought home," Sarah said, taking Ruthie's hand and heading toward the back door.

"See you in a coupla hours," Cameron said, leaning down to give Ruthie a goodbye kiss. Peyton waggled her fingers to Ruthie who waved back as she skipped away.

"Baby chicks, Miss Sarah! Baby chicks!" Ruthie squealed with joy.

Back in the truck, Cameron got back on the highway and drove past the entrance to Greyson. About a half mile later, he turned down a dirt road which threaded between two fields planted with knee-high stalks of corn. When the corn fields ran out, the road narrowed, twisted and traveled through dense pine forests threading its way toward the river. At the end of the lane stood a portion of a chimney stack, the front façade of one tenant house and another one, still standing but completely covered with kudzu vines. Peyton remembered hearing her parents say that a house servant, a family cook, had resided there as recently as the 1940s, She got out of the truck, carefully made her way onto the porch and peered inside the dusty window frame. "Look, Cameron, they papered their walls with newspaper. Some of these date from the thirties."

"Yeah, times were pretty hard around here for a lot of folks. They made do with whatever they had."

They walked around the ruins, tracing the foundation walls of the old houses. White oaks, walnut trees and small pines grew up out of piles of broken foundation bricks.

"We probably better get back in the truck. I saw a copperhead around here the other day."

That was all Cameron needed to say to convince Peyton she belonged in the truck. She hastened back, climbed in the front seat of the truck and buckled up, shutting the door with a bang.

Cameron got in, turned the truck around and continued down the narrow dirt road for another quarter mile through fields of corn and peanuts. The large limbs of oak trees shaded the lane and brushed the sides of the truck windows. Once, Cameron had to stop to remove a fallen limb from the road. Weeds were everywhere and an abundance of honeysuckle and overgrowth practically obscured their path.

Suddenly, the truck rounded a bend and Peyton drew in her breath at the sight of two tall brick pillars announcing a drive surrounded by the most impressive trees she'd ever seen.

"Oh my gosh," she cried. "What in the...?"

"Yeah, takes your breath away, doesn't it?"

Stretched out before the pair lay a vast expanse of green whose perimeter was shaded by twenty huge oaks, ten on each side. The heavy arching limbs of the oaks once shaded various outbuildings, now lost to time. At the end of the oaks sat a two-story Federal style house of brick, with white marble quoins and trimmings. Shutters on all the windows, some hanging loosely, wanted a coat of paint badly. Two tall square chimneys rose from the roof at either end. Stretching to the east of the once lovely manse, a gravel-covered path led to four small houses.

The main house itself, half the size of Greyson, was sadly in disrepair on one side. Bricks from the top of one of the chimneys lay scattered on the ground near the house. White pillared porches, one atop the other, announced the entrance to the grand old house. But portions of the roof had fallen in and signs of water damage were everywhere.

Cameron drove the truck up the lane and pulled to a stop near the front entrance. He got out, cautioning Peyton to watch her footing as she exited the cab. They stepped cautiously onto the front porch and turned to look again at the magnificent rows of oaks.

"I've just never seen anything so lovely," she said, turning back to the house.

Peyton stood on tiptoe to look inside a window. There, furniture sat draped in dirty muslin drop cloths. She stepped off the porch, walked to the side of the house and called Cameron to follow her. Nestled next to the walls of the house were overgrown shrubs and lilac bushes. Brick paths laid in a herringbone pattern surrounded the house and led behind the house. There, a winding path covered in more herringbone-laid bricks led down the hillside to a dock which teetered uncertainly in a shallow creek.

"What is this?" Peyton whispered.

"This is the place old Thomas Grey built for himself ten years after he lost the main house. He called it The Refuge. They say he drank himself to death down here, after the death of his wife Louisa. It's pretty amazing, isn't it? I'm not sure there's anything worth saving in the old house now. It's been pretty beaten down by storms. I haven't seen the inside in a good while. But I think the house exterior and foundation are solid. "

Cameron took her arm to steady Peyton as she tripped on a root which had come through the walkway and led her back to the front yard.

"The reason I brought you back here was to show you these oaks," Cameron said, gesturing to the twenty oaks around the front lawn.

"Taylor Jamison has had his eye on this property for quite a while. I heard he had a timber cruiser looking over these trees. He wants to buy this plot, cut down the trees and subdivide the land. He's planning a subdivision here that he thinks will bring in the DC commuters. It's only about an hour and a half into town if you take the greenway."

"But that's…that's impossible. Why, these trees must be 200 years old. You can't cut 'em down."

"More like three hundred. But that's what he wants to do."

"Why doesn't the owner do anything? Who owns this property, anyway?"

"You do, Peyton, for now."

It took Peyton a minute to understand that this beautiful spot belonged to her. She shook her head and looked around in disbelief.

"You don't understand, Cameron. I grew up at Greyson. This place is only a couple of miles back in the woods. Why didn't my mama and daddy ever tell me about it?"

"Well, it didn't really come into their hands until a couple of months ago and it was posted with lots of "No Trespassing" signs before then. Your daddy's great uncle owned the place and Mr. Jimmy inherited it when his uncle died. Your parents had mentioned fixin' the old house up for a hunting and fishing lodge but just never got around to it. One of the last conversations I had with your folks was about that very thing. Your daddy asked me to start looking for local contractors who had experience with historic houses. I think he wanted to maintain all the old details of the house, but bring it up to code. Your mama talked especially about upgrading the kitchen and adding a bathroom. Two months ago we had a bad storm that tore a portion of the roof off. I don't know if anybody ever came back here much when your daddy's great uncle owned this place. But I drive back here every once in a while to check up on it. Seems like I can't forget about these trees.

"I think Taylor's probably gonna try to horse trade with you for this property. You know – he'll offer to refinance your loan at a very low rate and cut the principal debt some just to get this. I don't think he knows you know about it, so he'll probably try a blind offering. What'll you do?"

"Well, he can't do that. He just can't. These trees couldn't be replaced in a hundred years – two hundred," Peyton exclaimed.

She took a few steps and looked around her, eyes wide open in amazement.

"Are we farming any of the land around this place, Cameron?"

"Not since Mr. Jimmy got it and I don't think they did for a long time before that... Your daddy just never got around to it. The fields would've had to be worked pretty good to get them ready for planting. But the place has excellent spring water, and good soil. "

The pair stood quietly looking around them. A tear came unbidden to Peyton's eyes and she looked up into Cameron's eyes.

"My mama and daddy left a big hole when they died, didn't they? You don't really realize what wonderful parents you had until they're gone, I guess. "

"You'll never know. I don't have parents of my own. I spent my teen years in a foster home near Charlottesville after my folks died. I got into Agriculture College on a scholarship and then was lucky enough to get a job here. When I came to work for Mr. Jimmy and Miss Dorothy, they kinda took me under their wings. Treated me like I was their own son. Maybe I don't have a right to say anything but I'd hate to see everything they worked for lost. They were remarkable stewards of this land."

Peyton dissolved into sobs then and Cameron reached an arm around her shoulder. She turned into his chest and tucked her head into his neck. They stayed locked in this embrace for maybe two minutes until Peyton straightened her shoulders and looked up at him again.

"I'm glad Mama and Daddy had you to depend on. I should have come home more. I'll always regret that. Thank you, Cameron, for being here for them."

"You'll never know what they meant to me, Peyton. They gave me a real start in life. And they loved Jane and Ruthie too – just like they were family." He kicked at the dirt with his boot and looked around. "I guess this'll give you something to think about now, won't it?"

Peyton nodded her head in silent reply and took another look at the oaks. The daylight was beginning to fade and shadows took the place of sunshine.

Cameron shook his head and resettled his cap, then said, "Let's come back another time when the light is better and we can poke around inside. We'd better head back and pick up Ruthie."

Peyton wiped the last tear from her cheek and looked up at Cameron with a smile. They got into the truck, looked around one more time, then headed down the long lane.

Chapter Nine:

Grey's Station

THE NEXT AFTERNOON BEFORE PICKING UP RUTHIE FROM THE Little Red Schoolhouse, Cameron turned the dusty pickup truck into the gravel-covered lane that led to his house. It was formerly the overseer's house on the Greyson plantation, and Dorothy and Jimmy Thurman had given it to Cameron and Jane in return for Cameron's thrifty stewardship of their farm.

The house itself was a small brick one-story dwelling that had been built on land once inhabited by the Weyanoke Indians, one of the largest groups of the Powhatan Native Americans. It was on this land that John Grey, the father of Thomas Grey, had traded with the Weyanoke for the plot of land on which Greyson now sat.

The brick house was the first house constructed in this area of the river and Thomas Grey's father, John, had proudly named it Grey's Station. He had run a small trading post in the original log building which had been next to the house. As his business prospered, he had acquired several hundred acres surrounding it. The trading post had become the center of commerce for the early settlers around what was to become the nearby township of Braverton Mill. Not far upriver from the trading post, a neighbor, Zechariah Braverton, had established a grain mill which gave the town its name.

When John and Bertha's son Thomas grew up, he had far grander plans than those of his father and made his fortune at sea. When he returned to Grey's Station with a chest full of gold, he told his father he'd never live under his roof again and proceeded to purchase a much larger tract of land four miles upriver, the place that he named Greyson. Meanwhile the elder Grey ran his trading post business until he was felled by a stroke which left him completely paralyzed on one side and unable to talk. His son, seizing the opportunity, forged his father's signature on the deed to his father's property and took over the trading post just three months before his father's death. His mother, now alone and destitute, soon followed her husband to his grave and the son's victory was complete.

With his parents gone, Thomas set out to enlarge his fortune and continued ferrying goods between London and the harbors along the east coast of the colonies. Soon he was wealthy enough to begin construction of his plantation manor house which he named Greyson. Shortly thereafter, he brought his wife Louisa into the manse.

When young Thomas moved into his new manor house, his parents' small brick home sat empty. The foot-thick walls laid in Flemish-bond brick still contained the original fireplace in the English basement. Wooden floors with hand-wrought nails where Grey's parents once walked now grew dusty with disuse. The roof of the log cabin where Thomas's father once traded with Native Americans fell in after a particularly brutal winter storm one year. Thomas had to repair it when he was forced to move back there after the loss of Greyson.

Two hundred years later, John and Bertha's house belonged to Cameron, a gift from his employers. Jimmy and Dorothy had modernized the house somewhat, adding central heat and air conditioning and giving the interior walls a fresh coat of paint, but since Jane's death, Cameron was hardly ever there. Just now, he pressed the ignition button on the dash to stop the engine and emerged from the truck. He headed over to a small barn at the rear of the house. There in the mixture of shadows and beams of sunlight was his hobby – a 1937 Allis Chalmers WC tractor.

Restoring that old piece of machinery and taking care of Ruthie had been the two things that had kept him sane in the months since Jane's death. He recalled the evenings he'd spent lying under the tractor putting on an oil pan or repairing a broken brake and smiled to himself. Night after night he'd followed the same routine – putting Ruthie to bed, making sure she was sound asleep with the baby monitor turned on, then heading out the back door to the barn for an hour or two with the tractor. He stopped his work every so often to check the baby monitor placed on a shelf near the tractor, then returned to whatever he was working on.

Cameron enjoyed the simplicity of the tractor's engine – no computers or metrics to worry about and plenty of room to move about. There weren't even many wires to deal with – just one for each spark plug. And he hadn't even had to buy many extra tools to work on the project – an important point because money was always tight.

He ran his hand lovingly over the tractor's giant left rear wheel, then turned to go back to the house.

"I'll finish you later," he said to the tractor.

Cameron walked around the yard, pausing to admire the daffodils Jane had planted. He walked up the three wooden steps and entered the front hall. Throwing his cap onto the table by the front door, he sat down at the desk in the front parlor, one of two small rectangular rooms that made up the front of the house. Rifling through the bills in the brass letter stand on the desktop, Cameron stopped and stood. He moved to a window on the back of the house and looked out to the river's edge. He picked up a pair of binoculars from a table nearby and focused on a bald eagle nest in a tree on the opposite shore. Unbidden, Peyton's face came into focus in Cameron's mind. He thought of the long waves of her chestnut hair and longed to pull his fingers through them. He imagined his arm around her trim waist and her brown eyes looking up at him. Deep in his loins he felt a pang of loneliness and longing that was almost unbearable, followed by guilt as he remembered Jane.

Suddenly, the phone on the desk jangled loudly, waking Cameron from his reverie. He picked up the handset. "Greyson" read the caller ID.

"Hey Cameron, it's Peyton – I got a call from Taylor. He wants to talk about The Refuge. I guess we better get together to plan our strategy. You want to come over for dinner tonight?"

"Nah, I can't. I gotta go pick up Ruthie from Miss Sarah's. And anyway, Ruthie is pretty busy at dinnertime. It wouldn't be much fun for you. "

"Are you kidding? This place could use a little noise. Why don't you bring her with you? I'll grill some burgers. I make the world's best macaroni and cheese. Ruthie can crash on the couch after dinner while we talk."

"Ok, but you were warned!"

Cameron hung up the phone and looked out the window again. Two bald eagles, a male and female circled the nest across the river, each carrying something in their beaks. He picked up his cap from the hall table, and headed out the door to pick up Ruthie at the Little Red Schoolhouse.

Four miles away at Greyson, Peyton headed through the dining room into the kitchen. She began thinking through her dinner plans, deciding that a meal served in the kitchen rather than the grand dining room would be best. She opened the refrigerator door and began pulling out ingredients for supper. Something like excitement stirred within her and she smiled a little.

Chapter Ten:

Dinner at Greyson

PEYTON SAT AT THE DRESSING TABLE BEFORE THE Chippendale mirror and ran a brush through her long brown hair. As she did so, she was mentally running through her menu for the night's meal. She made a list in her head of what she needed to do.

- *Glad I put the macaroni and cheese casserole together this afternoon.*
- *Get out toys for Ruthie*
- *Make hamburger patties*
- *Gather condiments and buns for burgers*
- *Make sure the grill is ready*

She looked at her reflection in the mirror debating whether or not to use her mascara. She decided against it, and then changed her mind. She applied a quick coat of lipstick to her lips, and then walked to her closet.

She opened the double doors, and then marveled again at her mother's amazing ability to organize. Dorothy Thurman had installed walk-in closets with matching polished wooden hangers in each bedroom at Greyson. On either side of Peyton's closet were shelves which held row upon row of shoes, purses and belts. Dorothy had insisted that Peyton leave plenty of her own clothes there so that on her flights home from London she wouldn't be burdened with too much luggage. After pulling out and then rehanging dress after slacks after shirts, Peyton selected a pair of white jeans and a blue oxford cloth button down shirt which she tucked in. She slipped her tanned feet into a pair of strappy brown sandals and threaded a brown leather belt through the loops of her jeans. Rolling up the sleeves of her shirt, Peyton closed the doors of her closet and headed downstairs for the kitchen.

She grabbed her mother's faded calico apron from a hook on the pantry door, slipped it on and tied it in the back. Then she pulled a dish from the refrigerator removing the foil covering to check it. She had just put that casserole dish of macaroni and cheese into the oven and set the timer when she heard a knock at the back door. Putting the oven mitts down, she wiped her hands on the towel on the counter, walked to the back door at the end of the center hall and pulled it open. There she saw Cameron heading back down the stairs. Ruthie was toddling off in the direction of the small pasture behind the house where two bay horses grazed under tall maple trees.

"Wait, Baby," Cameron called. "Wait for Daddy."

"Well, hey there," Peyton said, walking down the steps. "What's goin' on?"

"Ruthie just saw the horses as soon as we started up the steps and took off after them," Cameron said, grabbing his toddler and swinging her around joyfully.

"Well, let's go introduce her."

Grabbing some sugar cubes from the canister on the back porch, Peyton skipped down the steps and joined Cameron and Ruthie by the stone fence. The horses slowly made their way to the trio at the fence and held out their muzzles to be stroked. Peyton gave them each a sugar treat and scratched their coats.

"These two are getting pretty old," she said. "I learned to ride on Maudie here when I outgrew Dusty."

"Yeah, your mama had a real soft spot for her. She was always after me to keep her hooves trimmed and her coat clipped. I think she looked at Maudie and remembered you riding her."

Tears came to Peyton's eyes as she thought of her mother standing at the fence talking softly to Maudie and her daughter Skipper. She thought of how many times her mother must have done that.

"You've always been so good to my parents, especially since I left home."

"They were easy to be with. I really liked them a lot. Since my own parents passed away, they were the closest I had to a mama and a daddy."

Ruthie wriggled to get free from Cameron's arms and he turned her loose in the yard. She ran under a tall pine tree, and bent down to examine a roly poly. Picking it up between her chubby fingers, she was just about to give it a taste when Cameron rescued the bug and set it down.

"Nope, Ruthie, we don't eat bugs."

"Come on, let's go inside," Peyton said. "It's a little more kid-friendly in there."

Climbing the back steps two at a time, Cameron held Ruthie under his arm football style. Peyton smiled at Ruthie's giggles. Inside the kitchen, Peyton had placed a basket of her old toys, carefully washed and examined ahead of time, for Ruthie to discover. Cameron set Ruthie down on the polished heart pine floor of the kitchen and watched her as she walked unsteadily to the basket.

"This is really nice of you, Peyton. You should have let me bring something."

"Are you kidding me? You did. You brought Ruthie. I'd pay just to hear that laugh. She's really adorable."

"Yeah, she's somethin' else. Hey, why I don't I start the grill while you get the burgers ready.

"You've got a deal, buddy. Ruthie and I will take care of things inside."

Thirty minutes later on the flagstone patio by the back door, the hamburgers were sizzling noisily on the grill. Soon Cameron plated the burgers and carried them into the kitchen where Peyton had set the long farm table for dinner. She had placed Mottahedeh Blue Canton plates and white cotton napkins on the plain wooden surface of the table.

"I couldn't find my old high chair for Ruthie but I did find some books from the library to prop her up."

"OK but we better put a towel over them just in case. She can get kinda wild with her food, you know."

Dinner was unremarkable except for the easy way Peyton and Cameron had with each other. They laughed uncontrollably when Ruthie squeezed her food between her teeth. They talked easily about their respective pasts. After the meal, Peyton picked up Ruthie and took her to the sink to wipe her hands and face with a damp cloth. The two adults put the leftover food in the refrigerator and loaded the dishwasher with the dirty dishes. Peyton wiped the countertops clean and folded the washcloth over the ledge of the sink.

"Come on upstairs. I've got something to show you," Peyton said with a smile. She tucked Ruthie easily on her hip and led Cameron to the back staircase. Climbing to the third floor, she opened the door to a large room over 60 feet in length.

"Your daddy told me about this room, but I never came up here. It was the ballroom, wasn't it?"

"Yeah, Mama said it was THE place to go in the county for parties back before World War I. Take a look around. I even heard this room was used as a hospital during the Civil War. I brought up my old tricycle for Ruthie. Can she ride yet?"

Ruthie wriggled out of Peyton's arms and proceeded to show her dad and Peyton how adept she was at riding a tricycle. Her short legs pedaled furiously as she rode up and down the length of the room.

Meanwhile Peyton opened door after door of the anterooms pointing out the ancient hinges on the doors. The grand Palladian windows at either end of the ballroom brightened the room even though it was nearing dusk. Along the walls, photographs and paintings in heavy wooden frames leaned upright, stacked one in front of the other. Old wooden drawers from long-ago chiffarobes held dried flower petals, faded ribbons and ephemera.

"We're not really sure what these rooms were used for. Daddy thought they might have been fainting rooms for ladies or maybe a place to keep supplies or musical instruments. He said there were once 60 identical chairs along the walls of the ballroom. There were two grand pianos, one under each Palladian window. Wasn't it something?"

"It's pretty special. Looks like it could use a little work though."

"Yeah, there was a leak up here and some of the baseboard is rotten in that corner. There's always something to fix in a house."

Ruthie took that moment to turn over the tricycle and she set up a loud howl that reverberated in the empty room. Cameron picked her up, dried her tears and, wrinkling his nose, indicated that it was time for a diaper change. So the three went back down the stairs and headed to the kitchen.

Peyton found the diaper bag and offered to change Ruthie's diapers, but Cameron insisted he'd do it. After changing Ruthie's diapers, Cameron followed Peyton out onto the long back porch and sat in one of the eight heavy rockers positioned along its length. Holding Ruthie in his lap, he looked out over the pastures to left and right and down the hillside where the land met the river. Close to the ground, a thousand fireflies glowed on and off. Ruthie, tired from the exertions of the evening, soon fell asleep in her father's arms.

"Maybe I better go on home. Looks like Ruthie's down for the count."

"Oh Cameron, do you have to go just yet? It gets kinda lonely around here at night."

So they sat and rocked and talked for hours, until the stars came out and the night air began to chill their arms. Peyton got a blanket for Ruthie and they walked together to Cameron's truck. He buckled Ruthie into her car seat, and then turned to face Peyton.

She stood next to him and looked up into his eyes. Overhead, a multitude of stars twinkled and the moon cast a bright glow on Peyton's upturned face. A smile crossed her face and, impulsively, she gave him a peck on the cheek. Then, suddenly shy, she stepped back.

"Thanks, Peyton. It's the nicest night I've had in a long while," he said, tucking the blanket in around Ruthie's arms. "Call me tomorrow?"

"Yeah, I'd like that a lot. My appointment with Taylor at the bank is at 9 tomorrow morning. I'll call you when I get back."

Cameron started the truck's engine and pulled slowly away down the gravel drive. Peyton wrapped her arms around herself and looked up into the night sky, smiling.

Chapter Eleven:
A Meeting with Taylor

AT 8:59 THE NEXT MORNING, PEYTON PULLED INTO A PARKING spot near the front of the bank in Braverton Mill and got out of the truck. She smoothed the creases from her teal blouse and khaki skirt and straightened the strap on her brown leather heels. Walking purposefully through the glass front door, she greeted the receptionist and asked to speak to Taylor Jamison. Before she got the sentence out of her mouth, Taylor was coming toward her from his office.

"Hey, here, Miss Peyton," he called.

Taylor, a tall man with silver hair, had divorced his first wife Margaret after thirty-five years of marriage and was currently dating a widow who owned a large cattle farm near Leesburg. In addition to his banking duties, Taylor frequently mentioned that he was a major shareholder in a local development company, had extensive real estate holdings in Chicago and held shares in two local minor league sports teams. Around town, he was considered quite a catch for whoever finally landed him.

After his divorce, Taylor had bought The Oaks, a property of nearly a hundred acres with a main house that was modern in a boxy style and was rumored to have cost in the neighborhood of three million dollars. The house was surrounded by stacked stone fences and kept private by a mechanical gate, a subject that was bounced around the Schoolhouse Café frequently. The consensus around the tables there was that the property was pretentious. The main house was two stories tall and included walls of all glass which faced the distant Blue Ridge Mountains. It was a property of which Taylor was justifiably proud.

"Peyton, young lady, you get prettier every time I see you."

"Hey, Taylor," Peyton responded. "It's wonderful to see you again."

"I was sure sorry to hear about your mom and dad. They were good people. You know I always wanted to be paired up with Jimmy in bridge. He was a good bridge partner."

"Thanks, Taylor. I appreciate that. It's been really hard to be at Greyson without them." She paused for a moment, and then continued. "I need to talk a little business with you today. I understand I need to refinance the farm under my name now."

"Yes, that's the general idea; Lot of papers to be signed. But you know, I wonder why a young girl like you wants to be saddled with a big ole place like that, working in London and all. Have you thought about selling it? I've got a couple of ole boys who want to buy property in the county for a little project they're thinkin' about. I could probably get them interested in your land for a pretty good price."

"No I don't think so, not right now anyway. We better just proceed with the refinancing. I didn't know Daddy had any liens against the farm."

"Just a little bitty one - $100,000 he took out last year for some equipment purchases, I think," Taylor answered and shifted his eyes to the papers on his desk.

Taylor began shuffling through the stack of papers and pulled out a folder marked "Greyson."

"Here it is," he said. "We'll just sign this right here and you can be on your way."

"Well, no, I want to take a look at it before I sign anything. Why don't I just take this file home and I'll come back to see you later to sign it."

"Ok honey, I've made copies of all the Greyson papers for you here. Lemme just see one thing," Taylor said pulling a pink piece of paper from the file and returning the folder to Peyton.

"This was misfiled. It belongs in Peaches Campbell's file. You know she's selling her farm since she and Jack got divorced. Ever since we've been working on this get-together dinner for our commercial customers, everything's gone to Hell in a hand basket around here."

Peyton tucked the folder under her arm and got up to leave. Taylor came around his desk quickly and gave her a big bear hug. Peyton smiled weakly and turned to go.

"Don't be a stranger, now Peyton. Let's get all this mess cleared up real soon, ok?"

"Right," Peyton called over her shoulder as she left Taylor's office.

She couldn't help an involuntary shrug and a feeling that she needed a bath.

Getting into the truck, Peyton put her purse on the seat beside her, reached for her phone and dialed Cameron's number. It rang seven times with no answer so she hung up and began the drive home. In a couple of minutes, her phone's ringtone notified her of a call coming in. She pulled over to the side of the road, picked up the phone and answered. It was Cameron.

"Hey, did you call me?"

"Yes. I just got out of the meeting with Taylor and I feel like I need a bath. He really creeps me out. And you were right. Something's fishy about him. He told me that Daddy had refinanced his loan for an equipment purchase. He didn't say anything about the house and acreage he bought. A man in his position shouldn't have that kind of lapse in memory, should he?"

"You're right, Peyton. I wouldn't trust that old buzzard any farther than I could throw him."

"I need to look over the papers in the folder he gave me. Then I need to see you. OK?"

"Just let me know when. I'll be there."

Peyton started up the truck again and pointed it toward Greyson. It was good to have Cameron in her corner.

Chapter Twelve:

Bank Business

As the door swung closed behind Peyton as she left the bank, Taylor stepped over to the plate glass windows that were a front feature of the bank. He peered down the street, his eyes catching Peyton as she climbed into the truck. Waving to her in a friendly manner, he turned and walked back to his desk. He was in a cheerful mood and whistled quietly as he sat down in his plush desk chair.

"Miz Adams, come in here, would you, honey? I gotta a little job for you."

Alice Adams, Taylor's plump 60-ish secretary, had been with him as long as he had worked in the bank and was an extremely loyal and hard-working employee. She showed up at the bank every day before almost anyone else, including Taylor, and had the keys to all the doors. She walked over to Taylor's desk and sat down, pencil and notebook in hand.

"I've written up a little piece I'd like you to clean up so I can get it ready for publication in the next couple of weeks, "Taylor said, handing her a file folder. "I've got a photo to add but I'll get that to you later. You think you can do that for me, hon?"

"Of course, no problem, Taylor," Alice replied, tucking her pencil behind her ear. She gathered her voluminous skirts and stood. "Will that be all?"

"For now, yes. Just see if you can polish that up for me in the next coupla days."

"Sure thing."

Alice backed out of the office and headed to her own desk positioned just outside the door to Taylor's office. Settling herself at her desk, she opened the file folder which contained only a single sheet of pink paper. She scanned the paragraph she saw and began rewriting it in her head:

OUTSTANDING OPPORTUNITY TO OWN A PIECE OF HISTORY

THIS IS A ONCE IN A LIFETIME OPPORTUNITY TO OWN A GRAND HISTORIC PROPERTY, BUILT CIRCA 1820. THE MAIN HOUSE WAS A RESIDENCE FOR ONE OF THE AREA'S EARLIEST SETTLERS, AND SITS AT THE END OF A GRAND ALLEE OF TALL OAK TREES PLANTED BY THE ORIGINAL OWNER. THE PROPERTY WILL BE SUBDIVIDED INTO 20 MASTERFUL PROPERTIES WITH HOMES BUILT WITH HISTORY IN MIND. EACH HOME SITE WILL BE FROM FIVE TO TEN ACRES IN SIZE. EACH HOMEOWNER WILL BE AUTOMATICALLY INCLUDED IN MEMBERSHIP OF THE EXCLUSIVE OWNERS' GOLF CLUB WITH DINING PRIVILEGES IN THE CLUBHOUSE. OTHER AMENITIES WILL INCLUDE STABLES AND RIDING TRAILS THROUGH THE SURROUNDING WOODS.

FOR MORE INFORMATION, SEE TAYLOR JAMISON AT THE BANK OF BRAVERTON MILL, VA.

Alice hurried to her desktop and began typing away. Her mind raced to make sure she got everything just right for Taylor. Alice always wanted to please Taylor.

Chapter Thirteen:
Sunday Morning at Church

IT WAS SUNDAY MORNING AND PEYTON HAD DECIDED TO GO TO church, the first time since she had returned home. The last time was her parents' funeral and, although she looked forward to the peace that she knew would envelop her as soon as she crossed the threshold of the old stone church, the memory of the funeral made her sad. Dressing hurriedly in a linen skirt of cornflower blue with a sleeveless cream silk blouse and strappy blue high heeled sandals, she went downstairs to the kitchen to make a bowl of oatmeal and a pot of coffee. Finding no coffee, she poured herself a glass of orange juice and stirred her oatmeal.

She grabbed a seat at the long farm table in the kitchen, took a notepad from the heavy wooden desk and began making notes as she ate.

Things to Do

- Invite Cameron and Ruthie for supper
- Discuss meeting with Taylor
- Go grocery shopping- COFFEE!
- Go to Post Office to pick up mail.

Dabbing the corners of her mouth, she put the bowl and glass in the sink, ran a little water in them and grabbed the truck key from the hook by the door. She dashed back upstairs to brush her teeth. She was almost out the door of her room when she stopped, rushed back to the mahogany nightstand between the twin beds and grabbed a small black leather-covered Bible. *OK, Mama, I remembered.* Then she was on her way.

She drove her dad's pick-up truck slowly down the quiet rural back road which led to the stone church in the countryside. Turning in the pebble-covered driveway, she slowed to marvel at its elegant beauty. She remembered her weekly attendance in the church, her parents at her side, and sighed a bit.

Like many homes in the area, the church was constructed not far from a meandering creek, a tributary of the Potomac River. Surrounding the church were fields of crops – corn and soybeans and occasionally winter wheat. The church itself was constructed of Virginia sandstone with mortar made of lime from crushed oyster shells. Each of the two longer sides had four leaded glass windows. The roof was covered in slate. To the side of the church was a small cemetery surrounded by a stacked stone wall. Cedar trees surrounded the graveyard, their evergreen boughs shading the marble and granite markers within. The graves in the churchyard were both recent and ancient. The land for the cemetery and church had been donated by a local family late in the eighteenth century and it was easy to imagine how the church looked back then. Not much had changed in the years since the first burial. Within the cemetery's walls were the graves of Peyton's grandparents and the fresh graves of her parents. She touched the corner of her mother's lace-edged handkerchief to her eyes and blinked as she walked quietly into the building.

Inside, the church was a minor masterpiece with hand carved walnut pews, pulpit and columns. The pews were smaller than those in newer churches to fit the smaller physiques of early settlers. Several of those colonists were buried under the church's floor, their graves marked by marble slabs carved with their names. Behind the pulpit a gleaming brass cross hung on the wall. The organist was playing an instrumental piece, "Sheep May Safely Graze," as Peyton and the other parishioners took their places in the pews. She was struck by the thought that so many Virginians had sought shelter within these two-feet thick walls through the years. So many had prayed here for the safe return of their loved ones from places with names like the Wilderness, Gettysburg, Germany, Normandy, Korea or Vietnam.

Looking around, Peyton spotted Cameron's tall figure as he entered carrying Ruthie in her Sunday best. Cameron stopped at Peyton's pew and whispered, "Is this seat taken?"

A broad smile crossed Peyton's face as she scooted over to make room. The hour passed with scriptures, prayers, hymns and a homily and brought the peace that Peyton had sought. After the closing prayer, the minister descended the pulpit and walked through the sanctuary, pausing to shake hands with his parishioners. He stopped beside Peyton to offer again a word of condolence on the loss of her parents and to say how delighted he was to see her in the service. Ruthie squirmed and pulled at Cameron's arm. Then, dropping the doll she had brought with her, Ruthie scooted out the door while her father rushed out to catch up with her. The chase ended at the gate to the cemetery where Peyton caught up to them, carrying Ruthie's doll. Cameron picked up Ruthie, and then looked down into Peyton's eyes.

"This must be hard for you," he said quietly.

"I'm beginning to be used to not hearing their voices, but I guess I'll never stop missing them. It's nice to be able to visit with them here, though – the church grounds are so beautiful."

A tear came to Peyton's eyes and she leaned down to hide them. Cameron reached over instinctively and drew her to him. His shoulders hid her tears from the church-goers who were exiting the grounds. She wiped her eyes with the white handkerchief Cameron offered her and said,

"There. That's enough of that. It's about time for some lunch. Hey, there's a new McDonald's over in Leesburg. We could drive over and let Ruthie play in their playground. How 'bout it? Would you like that, Ruthie?"

"Yay!" was Ruthie's response.

Cameron added "Yay! Me, too. Why don't you leave the truck here and you can ride with us. We can pick up your truck on the way back."

"Sounds good."

They got in Cameron's truck which, Peyton noticed, had been washed for the drive to church. On the way to Leesburg, they passed mile after mile of magnificent northern Virginia countryside, old stone mills, fenced pastures where herds of Angus cattle or Thoroughbred horses grazed lazily. Soon the blue pickup pulled into the brightly colored parking lot of the McDonald's and the trio walked in. Cameron ordered burgers and fries while Peyton took Ruthie to the playground. All was well until Ruthie fell from the slide and got a nasty abrasion along her thigh. Acting instinctively, Peyton and Cameron rushed over and put their arms around her to comfort her. Peyton dried her tears and reached into her purse for a Band-Aid.

"Will this help, Ruthie?" she asked.

Ruthie nodded her head and struggled to stop crying. Cameron looked down in wonder at the two of them as Peyton applied the bandage. Ruthie was soon back at play and Cameron and Peyton sat down again at their booth. Both were silent for a minute as they watched Ruthie climbing and sliding.

"You know, I've really enjoyed reconnecting with you and getting to know Ruthie. You're a terrific father."

"Well, I do the best I can. But I've got to admit, it's been a lot more fun lately with you around. How come somebody as terrific as you doesn't have someone special?"

"Oh, I've just never had the time. Always been serious about my career, you know. I guess I didn't realize what I was missing, but seeing you with

Ruthie kinda changes my mind. I'm really digging the whole McDonald's vibe. In fact, I was thinking about asking you two over for supper tonight."

"Oh, man, that sounds great but I have to say no. I'm taking Ruthie to my sister's house for a couple of days. I'm supposed to have dinner with her tonight. She lives in Fairfax so I probably won't be back in time. I could bring you some dessert tomorrow, though. Sue makes some of the best sour cream pound cake you've ever eaten."

"Now that sounds like a deal."

"Yeah – have some coffee ready?"

"Definitely," Peyton said as she and Cameron gathered Ruthie's belongings.

Note to self, Peyton thought, *DEFINITELY pick up coffee!*

Chapter Fourteen:
An Unexpected Visitor

CAMERON AND PEYTON COLLECTED RUTHIE AND HER DOLL
and got back in the truck for the drive back to the church. The ride back was
mostly quiet but occasionally Peyton or Cameron would point out some
sight alongside the road – an old barn, a herd of cattle, a lone mule grazing
in a pasture beside a shed. Ruthie oohed and ahhed at the sights but little
by little she grew more and more drowsy. Finally, Cameron eased his truck
into the parking space beside Peyton's pick-up truck and silenced the motor.
Opening her door, Peyton turned to say goodbye to Ruthie and saw that she
had fallen asleep in her car seat. She put her finger to her lips and smiled,
looking into Cameron's eyes.

"See you later?" she whispered.

"Definitely," Cameron responded with a little wink.

As Cameron drove off in his truck, Peyton followed it with her eyes
until it was out of sight. Then she got into her daddy's truck, started the
engine and drove home.

Sunday afternoon seemed to last forever. Peyton moved from room to
room, looking at this and that, her memories practically bouncing off the
walls. In the library, she picked up a magazine and thumbed through it but
soon threw it down on the coffee table. She picked up the remote and moved

through dozens of channels on the TV looking for something to interest her but nothing seemed to work. Finally it was nearing nine o'clock and Peyton heard the crunch of tires on the gravel of the driveway outside. A slam of the vehicle's door let her know that someone had arrived. Maybe it was Cameron back early!

She went to the door and drew it open expectantly but there instead stood her banker, Taylor Jamison.

Dressed in a black sport coat, white mock turtleneck sweater and pants of tiny hound's-tooth check, the banker stood on the front porch with a huge bouquet of spring flowers in his hand and a wide smile on his face.

"Well, hey, Taylor, I wasn't expecting you."

"I'm your welcome wagon," he teased. Just a little something to say welcome back to the old place. Can I come in?"

"Well sure, but I have to warn you, dinner's already over."

Taylor came in confidently, his eyes scanning the paneling in the center hall.

"Isn't it kinda late for you to be out with work and all tomorrow?"

"Well, I just wanted you to know how much we'd all you missed you around here. Why, you haven't visited a whole lot since you took that job in London."

"Yes, it was a long way from home. I was able to get home two or three times a year but I mostly just spent time with Mama and Daddy when I got home."

Taylor's eyes flitted around the room as he listened to Peyton. Peyton noticed this right away and spoke guardedly.

"I've sure missed this old place."

"Yes, but it's probably gonna be too big for you now, I guess. When are you headed back across the pond?"

"You know, it's a funny thing. Now that I'm here, I'm thinking of staying. I forgot how much I loved it."

Taylor seemed to startle a little at that but quickly recovered.

"I've seen you hanging around with that Hill boy who worked for your daddy. Has he found himself something else to do yet?"

"No, why would he? He's got all the work he can handle around here."

"I just assumed this place might be too much for you so you'd think about selling it. You know, I could probably find a buyer for you real quick – in case you need to get back to your job."

"You know, Taylor, I've taken a leave of absence from my job so I'm not really under any pressure to get back 'across the pond,' as you say. And I'm thinking seriously about coming back here for good."

"Well, I guess you know best. But just don't forget what I said."

"I won't and that's a fact. Now thanks for the flowers, Taylor. I've got an early day tomorrow so I'm going to have to say goodnight for now."

Taylor handed Peyton the bouquet and said, "Hey, before I forget, I was talking to a couple of timber cruisers from MacLean Lumber the other day. They're interested in looking over some of the hardwoods on your property and said they might be interested in buying quite a few acres from you. Think about it. That could mean some pretty good money."

Peyton stared wordlessly at him, her thoughts returning to the twenty oak trees at the Refuge. She turned to the front door and opened it wide. Taylor hesitated a minute, then seemed to regain himself and nodded.

"Okey doke, Miss Peyton. See you in town soon, I hope."

He stepped out onto the porch and walked quickly to his Cadillac Escalade. He waved his hand with a flourish, started the big engine remotely, and got into the car. He backed up the Escalade, turned it around and sent a spray of gravel everywhere as he hurried down the drive.

Jerk, Peyton thought. *He's got his nerve showing up here unannounced. He's definitely got some mischief up his sleeve.*

She closed the door, tossed the flowers into a trash can and moved to the library where she sat in her father's red leather club chair. She slipped off her flats, put her feet up on the ottoman and mindlessly turned on the television. Flipping from channel to channel, she searched for something to occupy her mind. Finding nothing to suit her, she mashed the button and set the remote onto the table next to the chair. She spent the next hour looking through the books lining the shelves in the room. But her mind was not on the books.

I wish Cameron would call, she thought. Finally at 10:45 she decided to give up and go to bed.

Peyton climbed the stairs slowly. *I don't know why you're so depressed,* she told herself. *It's not like you have anything going on with Cameron. And with raising Ruthie, he's certainly not interested in taking on another complication!*

She stopped at the door to her parents' old bedroom and looked in. The large room, its windows and tall canopy king bed hung with red toile de Jouy, still seemed filled with the presence of her parents. The plastered walls, painted a warm cream color, featured paintings of James and Flora Thurman, the senator and his wife, bordered in heavy gold frames. She paused at the foot of the bed where her old cradle rested. Looking up, she saw her reflection in the gold framed mirror between the tall windows. Her mother's dressing table still looked the same – its sterling silver brushes and crocheted dresser scarf untouched by time. In the corner, the Lone Star quilt from her grandmother still rested across her mother's chaise lounge. Inside the closets, her mother's and father's clothes still hung, just as they'd left them before their fateful airplane trip. Peyton had so far been unable to do anything with them. She wondered if she ever would. Shaking her head, she turned and made her way to her bedroom.

"Time for bed, old girl."

Chapter Fifteen:

Inside The Refuge

THE SUN BROKE THROUGH THE CURTAINS AND CAMERON squinted, then looked at the clock on his bedside table. *6:00 Monday morning,* he thought. *I gotta get up.* Remembering that Ruthie was at his sister's house, he stepped out of his shorts, stretched and walked to the bathroom. Turning on the water in the shower, he began thinking of the chores he had to accomplish that day. The water splashed cold at first, then turned into a warm stream and Cameron plunged beneath it. He showered quickly, soaping up and then rinsing off under the warm water. Stepping out of the shower, he grabbed the towel from the towel rack beside the shower door and proceeded to rub himself dry. He then pulled on boxers, a pair of jeans, and a gray t-shirt. He scratched his beard and picked up dirty clothes and sheets from all over the room, tossing the sheet and night clothes into the hamper.

"You know what," he said to his reflection in the mirror, "one of these days, you've got to get it together. We gotta work on potty training and a regular laundry schedule. I don't know how much more of this I can handle."

Walking into the kitchen, he opened a cabinet door and was reaching for the giant box of Count Chocula when the telephone rang.

Seeing the caller ID of "Greyson," he answered, "Peyton?"

"Mornin' Cameron. I'm just up and wondered if I could drop by there in a bit. I need to talk with you," Peyton said hesitantly.

"Is everything ok?"

"Well, I don't know. I just need to see you."

"Well sure, come on. I've gotta throw some laundry in the wash but after that I'm free."

"I'm coming over then. Save me some Count Chocula."

Cameron dashed back to the bedroom, grabbed an armload of dirty clothes and sheets from the floor and stuffed them in the washer, then added a detergent tablet and turned it on. Back in the bedroom, he pulled the covers up on his bed and picked up a couple of Ruthie's stuffed animals by her crib.

In a matter of ten minutes, Peyton pulled into the drive and got out of the truck. She walked around to the back porch, walked up the five steps and turned to look at the fields around the house. The corn in the field to the left was knee-high. *Last night's rain was just what we needed,* she thought. She pressed her hands on the top rail of the three white rails surrounding the porch and took a deep breath. Then she turned and rapped sharply on the door. Cameron let her in and said, "Hey. What's up?"

"Hey, Cameron. How'd Ruthie feel about sleeping over at your sister's last night?"

"Are you kidding? She didn't even say goodbye. As soon as she saw her cousins, she took off like a rocket. Sue's been great about helping me with Ruthie since Jane got sick."

"She must be great. I'd like to meet her sometime."

"I'd like that, too. I think you two would really hit it off. So what's up this morning? You sounded funny on the phone."

"Yeah, it's been somethin' all right. First of all, last night Taylor came over – just before nine. He just showed up. And he brought flowers - total shock. I mean, I haven't seen him in five years. And, bonus, he's at least thirty years older than me. What is he thinking?"

"Yeah, I wouldn't worry about it. Taylor was just being Taylor. Besides he's probably got a couple of things on his mind," he said quizzically. He reached into the cabinet and grabbed two white coffee mugs in one hand, setting them on the table.

"So I guess it's too early to get in on that pound cake, huh?"

"Actually, I have a couple of pieces left. I debated eating it all last night but cooler heads prevailed. I've found it's the perfect accompaniment to Count Chocula."

Cutting a couple of thick slices of cake and pouring coffee into the mugs for both of them, Cameron smiled at her.

"I'm glad you came by this morning. I've got some chores to do but I could put them off for a bit. Want to go back over to The Refuge? It might help you make some decisions about your land. There's something I've been meaning to show you."

"That's exactly what I came over to talk about. Taylor did it. He actually said he knew some people who wanted to buy some timber. I just know he was talking about those big old oaks lining the drive. He mentioned that he'd heard from a timber company that they were interested in purchasing some hardwood and wanted to know was I interested in selling some of my timber. I mean, I just found out I owned 'em and now I have to think about selling them! And how'd those people even get on my property to know the oaks were there anyway?"

Cameron stood up involuntarily, a questioning look in his eyes.

"You're not actually thinking of selling the place, are you?"

"Well, no, I guess not, but why would he want it?"

"Who can figure out Taylor Jamison? And, other than the fact that those trees alone are worth thousands of dollars, it's a pretty big tract of land, nearly a hundred acres. Why don't we go take a look at it again? Then maybe you can know what you're dealin' with."

Finishing their cake and coffee, they hurriedly stacked the dishes in the sink. Peyton poured some dish soap in the water and washed them while Cameron dried and put them away. It was a nice comfortable feeling they shared and neither one was anxious to rush the chore. But soon the last dish was washed and dried and Cameron hung up the towel. He walked back to the laundry room, moved the clothes to the dryer and turned it on.

"OK, let's go, Peyton, before I see another thing that needs doin' around here."

Locking the back door behind him, Cameron put his hand lightly on the small of Peyton's back as he guided her down the steps. He opened the passenger door of his truck for Peyton and watched her swing her long jeans-clad legs into the seat. He walked around to the driver's side, started the pickup and headed the several miles to The Refuge. Instead of taking the back road through the fields as they had before, Cameron drove several miles on the main highway and turned at a signpost whose letters had long since faded. To the left was the path through the fields they had taken the other day. In front of them, almost hidden by overgrown bushes, a jungle of honeysuckle and weeds at the head of the drive, was a gate of ornate wrought iron, now rusted and hanging crooked. This gate was attached to square brick pillars whose stucco was almost all gone. Each pillar was about eight feet high and surmounted by a pineapple on top of a ball, now covered with dead vines. Cameron got out of the truck and unlocked a chain bearing a "No Trespassing" sign which hung between the pillars. Through the gates, the oak-lined drive led to the house. He drove the truck through the gate into the lane, then got out and replaced the chain.

Peyton was stunned again at the magnificence of the ancient gnarled oaks, lining the drive to the old house. They stood equally distant from one another and each spanned ten feet in girth. Incredibly, after so many years growing unattended, the trees were healthy and strong. Parking the truck beneath the long thick limbs of the oak nearest the house, Cameron and Peyton got out and walked around in silence.

"Can you imagine if whoever planted these so many years ago could see them now?" Peyton said in wonderment.

"I expect it was Thomas Grey, the original owner of Greyson. He thought he'd build up his fortune again and have another grand estate like Greyson. But he just went crazy when his wife Louisa died. He started drinking and he was dead a little while later. The place has been lived in off and on through the years but nobody ever really called it home. It's a shame, really. This place could be magnificent with a little work."

The house rose before them – a two-story brick mystery whose double porches shaded the shuttered doorways. Thomas Greyson had lived here in isolation, his only companions after the death of his wife being the slaves who served him.

"So what do you think I should do with it?"

Cameron waited a bit, measuring his words before he spoke.

"I think you should hold on to it. I think you'd be one hundred percent crazy if you sold this piece of ground and these trees. I think if it was mine, I'd look up to the Heavens and thank God every night for a place as beautiful as this to call mine."

"That's exactly what I've been thinking," Peyton said, a smile crossing her lips, "only I hadn't put it into so many words. I just don't know where to begin. So how do I keep Taylor and his buddies at the lumber mill from getting hold of all this?"

"I think we better just sit back and wait for Taylor to make his next move. And while we're waiting, let's poke around inside the house a little bit."

They walked up to the portico, tried the door and pushed their way in.

"You need to get a lock for this place, Peyton. I could call a locksmith if you want."

"Good idea. Let me know when and I'll come down here and wait for him."

"Not a good idea. This place is kind of remote so I'll come with you when the locksmith is here."

Inside the front door, the pair entered into a stair hall that was decorated with fabulous scenic wallpaper, water damaged in places, which ran up the mahogany staircase to the second floor hallway. The staircase newels and rails were handsomely carved though someone had painted them a vivid shade of pink. The downstairs hallway was wide, over ten feet, and extended twenty feet or more in length. At either end, double doors provided access to the front and rear porticoes.

"I'll bet these doors were open all the time in the summer. That's the way they used to cool off these old houses back before air conditioning," Peyton said, tugging the back door open. "Just look at the river out there, Cameron!"

She looked out at the river beyond the lawn, its waters now clogged with fallen limbs and weeds. Everywhere, nature's growth had overtaken Thomas Grey's original plan.

Cameron walked over to Peyton and put his hand on the molding atop the door. Out the back door was a wide gallery with marble steps leading to the grounds beyond. A hillside nearly as grand as the one behind Greyson ran down to the river below. On the lawn a grove of centuries-old tulip poplars bore witness to Thomas Grey's original plan. To the left of the rear portico stood several original outbuildings, a freestanding brick building that was the original kitchen, a laundry, an ice house, smokehouse, root cellar, carriage house, stables, and other buildings. To the right of the house lay the remains of a formal garden and a small cemetery whose stone fence was overgrown with honeysuckle.

"That's where old Thomas Grey is buried," Cameron pointed. "And beyond the cemetery about a half a mile is a group of old barns that belong to you, too. I haven't been back there in a while but they're still in pretty good shape, last I saw of them. Come on, let's see what's upstairs."

Peyton ran ahead of Cameron up the wide stairs and turned at the top to look down. She missed her footing and fell down three steps. Cameron was behind her in a flash and caught her in his strong, muscled arms. For a minute, neither of them spoke. Peyton was dangerously aware of a clinching inside her that signaled arousal, a feeling she wasn't expecting. She righted herself, laughed nervously and said,

"Woo, thanks Cameron. Almost lost it there. "

"Yeah, lucky I was right behind you."

He held a look right into her eyes for a minute longer than he should have, then said, "Are you sure you're all right?"

"Come on, I'm fine. Let's see what's up here," Peyton said looking into a bedroom door. She tried to appear nonchalant, but Cameron couldn't help seeing the blush in her cheeks.

The rooms on the north corner of the house had suffered some water damage as Cameron had told her but they were not beyond help. Collapsed plaster and slivers of skylight between the exposed laths gave evidence of the repairs needed. Wallpaper peeled from the walls and paint chips flaked off the elaborately carved cornices but Peyton could see what a classically simple and beautiful house it had been.

On the opposite side of the upstairs hall, Peyton found a large riverfront bedroom almost untouched by the years except for the dust. In a corner opposite the door, a mahogany full tester bed surveyed the room. Its acanthus leaf design was almost completely obscured by dust yet it was still magnificent.

A dust covered crocheted canopy was attached to the testers. A day bed rested at its foot. On the wall opposite the bed, an armoire of mahogany held clothes from past decades.

Through an open doorway Peyton spied a nursery with a tiny, child-sized bed on rollers. In a corner of the bed a china doll sat, its dress wrinkled and dusty but intact. In another corner, a cradle covered in dusty mosquito netting sat empty.

Peyton gasped as she saw the room but said nothing. She walked from room to room on the second floor, each holding some treasure, lost to the years. Cameron followed her as she examined each object, once stopping to right a chair that was turned over. Mantels held hurricane glass-covered brass candlesticks. Bedside tables held china plates and old newspapers.

Back on the first floor, few articles of furniture remained and those few were covered with dusty muslin sheets. There was a very handsome chimney piece in the parlor backed by rich black veined Italian marble. A cast-iron fireback looked to be original to the house's construction date. Above the mantel was a large deeply carved frame which held the shattered remains of a mirror. The dining room across the hall was of a generous size and must have once accommodated a table to seat twelve or more. An elegant plaster ceiling medallion in the center of the room had survived but the chandelier which had been centered there was long gone. Now only a bare light bulb on a cord was in its place.

A pair of French doors separated the dining room from a portico on the side of the house. Two large rooms across the back of the house completed the first floor along with some utilitarian rooms and a bathroom which had been added sometime in the early part of the last century. One of the utility rooms was a pantry, adjacent to the dining room where food was brought in from the kitchen building for final preparation before serving. In the early part of the twentieth century someone had installed a wall-mounted cast iron sink and three-burner electric stove here to serve as a kitchen. A trap door in this room led to a wine cellar in the basement where a wall of shelves held empty bottles. Cameron opened the trap door to peer in but suggested they wait to go down and investigate until they had a flashlight. Another room had been the office, where Thomas Grey had watched his fortune and his land holdings diminish. A fall-front desk and now-broken office chair of cherry wood sat against one wall. On the desk in a carved wooden frame was a sepia portrait of a young girl in a white lace dress.

"This place must have been truly beautiful," Peyton said. "I wonder if it's too late for it. You know, despite all the damage done to the Refuge by the forces of nature and the unchecked vegetation overtaking the lawn, the house's exterior and foundation seem solid."

"You know, sometimes the best things in life come about because they've been repaired after being broken – like houses or furniture…"

"Or hearts," Peyton thought and looked into Cameron's eyes.

Opening the heavy oak door, they stepped out onto the front portico once more and looked around them. Cameron pulled the door closed behind him and made a mental note to contact a locksmith. They walked down the steps together and paused at the bottom. Turning to look back at the door, Peyton opened her mouth to speak and Cameron bent his head down to her. His lips brushed hers and she drew in her breath. Time stopped. Peyton tilted her head back, her lips wanting more. Cameron's work-hardened hands slid down her spine and pressed her closer to him.

"Peyton," he said, his eyes looking into hers, "these last few weeks since you've been back home have been the happiest I've had since…well, since Jane died. I don't know if you feel anything or if I even have the right to ask you to feel something for me. But I just thought you ought to know how I'm feeling."

Swallowing hard, Peyton took a deep breath and said, "You know, Cameron, when I came back home after my parents' passing, I wasn't sure where my future lay. I was lost and all alone. But then you came along. You showed me what I have here and all of a sudden, my future looks a little clearer. The weeks I've spent with you and Ruthie have been wonderful."

"I haven't dated anyone since Jane died. I've wanted to be real careful about bringing someone into Ruthie's life. But with you it just sorta seemed natural. I think starting as friends helps a lot."

"Ruthie is a wonderful little girl. I could fall in love with her pretty easily."

"But how about her daddy? Do you think you might be able to fall in love with him?"

A sassy smile came onto Peyton's face and her eyes lit up. "I think that's entirely possible. But not on an empty stomach. Isn't it about time to pick up some lunch?"

"Girl, are you always hungry?"

"Pretty much."

Cameron threw his tanned arm around Peyton's neck and pulled her to him for a squeeze. They grinned at each other, and then walked to the truck.

Chapter Sixteen:
The Barn at Night

THE MOON WAS FULL AND THE SKY WAS BLANKETED WITH A million stars. Taylor Jamison looked up through the windshield of his black Mercedes CL600, the second of four cars in his stable of premium vehicles, and smiled to himself. *It's a beautiful night,* he thought to himself. Turning the burled walnut steering wheel so that the coupe steered into the drive, Taylor turned off the radio and extinguished the headlamps. *Moonlight's enough tonight,* he thought.

Driving slowly down the narrow dirt path, Taylor looked around constantly for signs that anyone had followed him. Passing the looming hulk of The Refuge, he maneuvered his coupe down an even narrower dirt road behind the cemetery. Pulling up to the barn farthest from the house, Taylor cut the power to the car's engine and sat quietly for a minute on the cognac leather seats. He exhaled deeply and withdrew an expensive cigar from his pocket. He lit it and quickly extinguished the match.

Looking around him, he pocketed a small flashlight, exited the car and walked quickly to the large sliding door of the barn. Withdrawing a key from his pocket, he slipped it into a padlock on the door and walked into the barn. Striding to a hay bale that sat in the middle of the barn's open space, Taylor lit the flashlight which cast a weak glow over the barn's interior.

Looking around him, Taylor saw with satisfaction that everything was where it should be – Two large Chevy Suburbans had been painted a dull black. Stacked against a wall behind them were two boxes containing a dozen or more license plates from different states and several coils of rope. To the right were four pull-behind tanks holding 10,000 pounds of various gases. On a flatbed trailer just to the left of the tanks were 2,000 pounds of bagged fertilizer. On another trailer nearby were 800 pounds of bagged chemicals.

The chemicals before him were those normally used in fertilizers but no farm anywhere had them in the amounts in the barn at The Refuge. Since the terrorist attacks of 9/11, the Department of Homeland Security had put into place a screening system to safeguard supplies of fertilizers, pesticides and other chemicals deemed "high risk." Farmers in the area had had to complete a vulnerability assessment earlier in the year to determine if their supplies were at risk for theft.

"Thank goodness my boys got this stuff out before the screening," Taylor chuckled to himself. He laughed silently as he remembered how easy it was to haul the chemicals from Wally Peterson's barn on his farm off route 27 and the Whitley farm on the other side of the road. He'd watched as his boys, as he liked to call the migrant workers from Mexico and El Salvador, loaded the chemicals into the vans and the eighteen wheeler he'd repossessed from a farmer whose payments on his farm loan were in arrears. The chemical movement, done on a dark night some three weeks before, had been the last piece of his master plan for his "retirement" – a move to the south of France, a new name and a new life.

The bank thought I'm approaching retirement age, did they? Well, I'll show them – I'm nowhere near ready to slow down. Job one was to jettison that widow who'd been hanging around him, then look for someone a little more to his taste, someone considerably younger and prettier. Perhaps a little French mademoiselle would do the trick. The half million dollars he'd been promised for the chemicals from his contact, Carlos, should just about be enough to get him going, he thought to himself and grinned.

Taylor heard the slow crunch of a truck's tires on the rocks and dirt of the lane and automatically ducked. He threw the cigar onto the dirt floor of the barn and extinguished it quickly with his shoe. He edged over to the barn's door and peered through the crack. Not to worry – it was Carlos.

Carlos Delgado was a Salvadoran immigrant who had a police record as long as his arm. Mostly it was for small time drug offenses and breaking and entering. But now, Carlos had it in mind to make a big score by moving some chemicals. And he had tapped that shady banker Jamison to do the heavy lifting – locating, stealing and storing the chemicals until he, Carlos, was ready to make the sale. He'd been talking online with several potential overseas customers and he was getting excited.

A tall, powerfully built man, Carlos got out quietly from the pick-up truck and walked to the barn door. Giving a little low whistle, he opened the door and slipped in. Taylor motioned him in and quickly closed the door behind him.

Few words were exchanged but few were necessary as Taylor simply pointed out the chemicals in their various locations.

"So when are you going to pick it up?" he inquired in a low voice. .

"It'll all be gone by next week," Carlos replied. "Can you get more? I may have more than one buyer."

"I doubt it. I've got another game in mind – a little land deal I'm working. I'll let you know, though."

"OK, here's the first payment," Carlos whispered in a husky voice. He handed Taylor a manilla envelope bulging with $50 and $100 bills. "You'll get the second half when I pick this up. I'll let you know when."

"These better be real. You know I'll be checking them at the bank. Taylor said, as they walked back to the door. "You know how to reach me."

Carlos walked noiselessly to his truck as Taylor padlocked the door to the barn.

Now if I can just get that stupid little Thurman girl to sell me the property, Taylor thought to himself. He walked quickly over to the Mercedes, opened the door and slid in. The engine purred upon ignition and Taylor turned the car around. He drove back down the dirt lane, the headlights still off.

One hour later, Taylor was in his study turning the dial on a safe he had hidden behind a large painting of a corn field. He reached inside his jacket pocket and withdrew the envelope full of money, placing it securely within the safe. He gave it a little pat before closing and locking the safe door.

"That's a good night's work, Taylor, old boy," he chuckled to himself.

Chapter Seventeen:
A Telephone Call

CAMERON PULLED RUTHIE'S NIGHTGOWN DOWN OVER HER head, her brown curls bouncing as she jumped on the changing table.

"Whoa, Hoss, you better slow down. You might just fall off this table. You don't want a boo-boo, do you?"

Ruthie grinned as Cameron picked up his little daughter and carried her tucked in the crook of his arm to the rocker near her bed. "What book do you want tonight?" he asked, knowing full well what her answer would be.

"Little Engine," she said, wriggling free to retrieve the book from her shelf. She climbed up into Cameron's lap and settled herself into his arms, opening the book. "Wead," she ordered.

It was a book they'd read together nearly every night for the past six months, a routine that seemed to comfort Ruthie. Occasionally she selected other books but at least three out of seven days of every week, Ruthie wanted to hear The *Little Engine That Could.* So Cameron read, as requested.

"OK, Butter Bean, I'll 'wead.'"

He paused as he finished the book and smelled the clean fresh scent of his daughter's hair, her ringlets curling around his finger. Soon her breathing slowed and she went limp in Cameron's lap. After rocking her for a few minutes until he was sure she was asleep, Cameron eased himself out of the chair. He lifted her into her crib and covered her with the quilt Jane had made for her.

"Sleep tight, Sweetness," he whispered and tiptoed out of the room. "I love you."

He walked into the kitchen and ran a glass of water under the kitchen spigot, swallowing it all in two gulps. Going into the family room, he picked up the handset to the portable phone. Punching in the number for Greyson, he settled into the recliner and lifted his feet.

"Hello?" Peyton answered.

An involuntary smile crossed Cameron's lips as he heard her voice.

"Hey… it's me. You too busy to talk?"

"No. In fact, why don't you and Ruthie come on down for some ice cream?"

"Can't. I just put her to bed. She was exhausted – they were doing gymnastics at the Schoolhouse today. Miss Sarah said she was turning somersaults for hours after that," Cameron grinned.

"I'd like to have seen that," Peyton answered. "She's a real cutie."

"Yeah, she's something else. And Miss Sarah is amazing with her."

"You're pretty lucky to have Ruthie. Sometimes I wish I hadn't been so focused on my career. I think I missed a lot by not marrying and having children."

"You sound like you're a hundred years old. It's not too late for you to do all that," Cameron replied, then paused. "I've been thinking a lot about the things we said when we were together last. I hope I didn't speak out of turn and I hope you meant what you said."

Peyton thought for a moment, replaying their conversation in her mind before she spoke.

"You know, Cameron, it was almost unimaginable for me to come back to this big house without my parents here. I was sure I'd be gone within a month after I came back – you know, just clean it out and sell the place. I was pretty involved in my job in London and I didn't think I could bear to live here without Mom and Dad. But somehow, having you around made the pain easier to bear. Meeting Ruthie, though – well, that sealed the deal. She's amazing."

"She's pretty crazy about you, too. All she talks about is going to see Peyton again. To be honest that's pretty much all I think about now, too. How about breakfast with me in the morning? We could take Ruthie to the Café and then drop her off at Miss Sarah's. Then we can figure out where we're going from there."

"That sounds like an outstanding idea. How does 7:30 sound?"

"Perfect. I'll pick you up."

Cameron ended the call and put his phone back on the table, but he couldn't seem to wipe the smile off his face.

Over at Greyson, Peyton was having the same problem.

Chapter Eighteen:
Breakfast at the Cafe

AT 7:30 ON THE DOT, CAMERON PULLED INTO THE DRIVE leading to Greyson. He noticed a couple of areas where the stone wall at the entrance needed repairs and made a mental note to mention it to Peyton. Ruthie sat in the car seat and was singing off-key at the top of her lungs. Cameron couldn't help thinking of how happy he was. It was the Fourth of July. The sky was blue, the birds were chirping, crops looked good, his baby girl was healthy and he was picking up the woman he was beginning to believe might hold the key to his future. Life was good.

After parking under the shade of an overhanging oak tree, he emerged from the truck, and opened the back door. Unbuckling Ruthie from her car seat he set her down on the ground where she immediately grabbed a dandelion. Then she took off, toddling toward the house.

Peyton had been dressed and ready to go for a half hour. She had looked out the kitchen window, waiting expectantly for 7:30. As soon as she heard Cameron and Ruthie climbing the steps to the back porch, she opened the door and squatted down to be on eye level with Ruthie.

"Hey, pretty girl, ready for some breakfast?" Peyton said.

Ruthie responded by nodding her head vigorously up and down and handed Peyton the dandelion she'd picked from the lawn. Tucking her chubby hands in Peyton's and Cameron's, the three walked into the kitchen.

"Thank you, honey. Let's just get this in some water before we go," Peyton said withdrawing a glass from the cabinet and filling it with water. She put the dandelion in the glass as if it were the most delicate orchid. "There," she said setting it on the wooden table. "Perfect. Now let's go get some breakfast!"

The three walked down the steps of Greyson, pausing for a moment to look at Maudie and Skipper. Peyton promised to take Ruthie for a ride on Skipper soon and they headed toward the blue truck. A few minutes later, they pulled into a parking space a half block down from the Schoolhouse Café. Cameron unbuckled his daughter from her car seat and tucked her onto his hip.

"Guess everybody's in town for the parade and fireworks later on today. You wanta go with Ruthie and me?"

"That sounds like fun! I'd love to. I've just got to stop by the bank this morning to see Taylor. He's got some papers for me to sign."

"The bank's closed today for the Fourth, isn't it?"

"Taylor said he would be in his office for a few minutes so I could get the refinancing started."

"You better read those papers over real good before you sign 'em," Cameron warned. "There's definitely some shady stuff going on."

"Hmmm, are you sure you're not just jealous 'cause I've got another man who brought me that BEE-YOU-TI-FUL bouquet of flowers?" Peyton said and made a funny face at Ruthie.

Ruthie collapsed in her father's arms laughing at Peyton's silly face and Peyton pretended to be surprised.

"Oh, so you think I'm funny, huh?" Peyton said as she made another silly face for Ruthie. Ruthie took Peyton's face in her two dimpled hands and they both giggled. Entering the café, they slid into the first booth by the door and looked back at the owner.

"Since I appear to be the only adult around here, I think I'll order for everybody," said Cameron, adopting a mock-serious face. "Chub, where's Miss Emmaline this morning?"

"I gave her the day off. She's making jelly. What'll it be?"

"Blue plate specials for everybody?" Cameron said, looking around the booth. "I'll finish up whatever Ruthie doesn't eat."

Peyton and Ruthie both nodded vigorously.

"Your daddy's gonna get big and fat that way," Peyton whispered in Ruthie's ear. Ruthie giggled again.

"Hey, none of that secret stuff around here."

"Yeah, he's right Ruthie – we shouldn't be telling any secrets."

Ruthie took the crayons Chub offered her and proceeded to draw what she insisted was a chicken. Peyton and Cameron looked at each other over Ruthie's head and shook their heads, unable to see a bird anywhere. It was not long before Chub emerged from behind the counter bearing their food.

"Hey, look here, Ruthie," Peyton said, rubbing her hands together. "Here's our breakfast already."

Chub brought out a huge aluminum tray filled with three plates full of breakfast delicacies – country ham, scrambled eggs, bowls of grits swimming in butter, biscuits so light they could almost float, cups of juice for the adults and milk for Ruthie.

"Coffee now, folks?"

"Yes, please," Peyton said. "The sooner the better!"

Cameron began cutting up Ruthie's eggs into bite-sized pieces when Ruthie stopped him.

"No, Daddy, Peyton do it."

"Well, I guess I've been replaced," he said with a smile.

Breakfast was a happy affair, Ruthie singing in between bites while the adults laughed and finished the meal before them. When it was over, Peyton and Cameron both fought for the check but Cameron eventually won.

"I told you I'll let you pay when we go someplace much more expensive," he said, winking.

"Well, at least let me leave the tip."

"OK, but make it a big one. I'm known around town as a sport – I like to be generous, especially with someone else's money!"

Cameron scooped up Ruthie and followed Peyton out the door, calling to Chub, "I'm gonna pick up that pie I ordered later."

Chubb nodded and threw up his hand in reply.

The drive to Miss Sarah's Little Red Schoolhouse was brief and when they stopped, Ruthie was almost ready to jump out of the car seat.

"Look, Daddy, a pony."

Sarah's husband Walter had brought up Baby, his grandson's pony, for his wife's charges to ride this morning. He was standing under the shade of a maple tree, saddling the little fellow, who waited patiently.

"OK, Butterbean, I'll see you in a little bit," Cameron called to Ruthie. Ruthie ran to Sarah who was waiting with a child-sized helmet.

"Stand still, Baby, let me get this helmet on you," Sarah said. "OK, Cameron, same time?"

"Yeah, probably. I'll call if there's a change."

Cameron and Peyton then drove back into town, parking in front of the bank. Cameron looked at Peyton with a serious expression.

"I'm not sure about all the details of what Taylor's got up his sleeve but I just don't trust him. You going in alone or do you want me to go in with you?"

"No, I think you're right. Please go in with me? Let's throw him off his game a little bit."

Squeezing his arm a little, Peyton got out of the truck and walked quickly beside Cameron. He held the door open for Peyton and they entered the empty bank. Taylor was leaning over Alice Adams, his private secretary. Alice looked up as Peyton and Cameron walked in.

"Hey, here. If it isn't Peyton? And you've brought your hired man with you," Taylor called out, straightening and reaching a hand over the brass gate.

"Hey, Taylor. Cameron and I came in to sign those papers you were talking about. I stopped in last week to return the Greyson file. Miss Alice gave you that file I borrowed when I was in to talk to you recently, didn't she?"

"Why, of course she did, honey. Thank you for bringin' it back. Well now, we don't need Cameron. Why don't you step back here into my office? Good to see you again, Cameron," he said, dismissing him.

"If you don't mind, Cameron's coming with me."

"Oh...well... if you like."

Peyton watched carefully as Taylor withdrew a sheaf of papers from a file folder in his gray metal filing cabinet behind his desk. Handing them to her, he said," Now Honey, if you'll just sign these right where the X's are, we'll have all this business put in your name."

"You know, Taylor, I'm pretty new at all this. If you don't mind, I'd like to have a lawyer look at this. Do you mind if I take them home with me? I don't want to make any mistakes."

"I don't see why you have to worry but if it makes you feel better, why, go right on ahead. Are y'all going to the fireworks later on?"

Cameron stood and steadied Peyton's chair as she got up.

"Yep, probably so, Cameron drawled. " Be seein' ya, Taylor. Guess Miss Peyton has more chores for me to take care of."

He put his hand on the small of Peyton's back and guided her through the door, trying hard to keep the smirk off his face.

When they were safely back in the cab of the truck, Peyton snatched Cameron's cap and smacked his shoulder with it.

"You almost got me laughing in there. He's gonna suspect we're onto him."

"Well, we kind of are, aren't we? We just don't know what it is we're onto yet."

Chapter Nineteen:

Fireworks

THE MORNING PASSED QUIETLY ENOUGH WITH CAMERON going back to his place to do a little more work on his Allis Chalmers and Peyton staying at Greyson to look over the new forms from Taylor. She scanned the forms and sent them on to Adam Thomas, her attorney at the law firm of Elliott & Bond to discuss what she was reading. Adam had been her parents' attorney for twenty years and had handled anything she needed since graduation. Peyton trusted him implicitly just as her parents had. After texting Adam about the scans and giving him time to look them over, Peyton waited nervously for his response. What she learned when Adam called her didn't please her.

"Peyton," Adam said. "This just doesn't add up. Your bank president says he's got a potential buyer for your mama and daddy's place, and yeah, I guess the figure he's got in there is fair, but I don't get it. Why is he pushing this? There doesn't seem to be anything in it for him. I'd hold off on signing anything till I can do a little more research."

"Yeah, I agree, Adam. Cameron and I can't get a read on him either."

"Cameron Hill? Is he still there? I knew him when he first came to work for your parents. He graduated from Virginia Tech with an Ag degree, didn't he? Give him my best. He's a fine man."

"Yeah, I think so, too. He's really been a big help to me this summer. In fact I probably would have been back in England by now if I hadn't had his help. How's Lucinda? Will we see you two at the fireworks tonight?"

"Maybe. She isn't back from Tyson's Corner yet. They had a big sale at Nordstrom's, so I think my credit card is probably steaming right about now."

"I expect so," she said laughing. "Well, thanks for the information. We'll see you if we see you."

Replacing the phone in the dock, Peyton sat and stared at it for a minute. Then she picked it up again and called Cameron.

Cameron pulled his cell phone out of his jeans pocket and checked to see the ID. Seeing "Greyson" he immediately answered, "Hey. What's up?"

"Hey, I just talked to Adam Thomas. I scanned him the papers Taylor gave me. He thinks that moron is trying to pull a fast one, but he can't quite figure it out yet either. He said just to sit on the papers for a while until he's through looking them over."

Cameron rubbed his forehead with his palm and nodded. "Good thinking. I want to take another crack at them myself. Hey, you up for the fireworks at the community center tonight?

"I was hoping you'd ask. I haven't seen a good old Fourth of July celebration in quite a while. You know, oddly enough they don't celebrate that over in London! Pick me up after dinner?"

"Yeah, around 7:00 – the parade starts at 8:00 so we can get a good spot."

Hanging up his phone, Cameron paused for a moment as Ruthie's face came into his mind. He realized just how loud the fireworks were going to be and he pictured his little girl's reaction to them. Just then Sue called, breaking into his thoughts.

"Hey, Sis! What's up?"

"Hello, you old renegade. What's going on out in the sticks?"

"Not much. I'm going to the fireworks display tonight with Ruthie."

"Just Ruthie?" she replied, a smirk in her voice.

"Well, I thought I'd ask Peyton to go with us."

"Hey, I've got a better idea. Let me come pick up the little squirt for a spend-the-night with Charlie and me. The kids would love to have her and the fireworks would probably scare her anyway."

"I know what you're doin', Sue. Always playing matchmaker. But you know, you're probably right."

"Ok, I'll be over in an hour or so to pick her up."

Cameron pressed the end button on his cellphone and replaced it in his pocket. He began whistling softly.

After a supper of leftovers from the refrigerator, Peyton went to her room and opened the closet doors. She selected a fresh pair of jeans and a red t-shirt. She slid her feet into a pair of red high top Chuck Taylors and then tied her hair back into a ponytail. Brushing her teeth and slicking on some gloss, Peyton skipped down the stairs to await her ride.

Soon the sound of Cameron's truck caught her attention and she opened the back door. Grabbing her keys from the counter Peyton went out the door, and locked it behind her. She walked over to the truck and reached over the fence to scratch Maudie's muzzle before getting in the cab.

"Where's Ruthie?" Peyton said as soon as she opened the door.

"My sister came over and picked her up. Sue thought it might be too loud for Ruthie, so she's having a little sleepover with her kids."

"Yeah, I guess it might be a little scary. Too bad. She'd have liked the colors."

"Well, maybe you and I can spend a little time together tonight if you'd like."

Peyton's heart did a little skip as she looked at Cameron's smile. He reached across the seat and took her face in his hands. Leaning toward her, he kissed her softly and quickly, then pulled back and looked in her eyes. Peyton blinked and swallowed.

"Not ok?"

"Yes, oh yes," Peyton answered. "Very ok. I think my heart rate just went up about a thousand beats per second, that's all."

"Then I guess we better stop these fireworks and get over to the ones the town's putting on."

Cameron gave Peyton's hand a quick squeeze and started the truck engine. The drive to the community center was short, too short in Peyton's opinion. She could have looked at Cameron's long arms stretched out to the steering wheel forever.

You are getting seriously stupid about this guy, she told herself, and a goofy grin played around her lips.

"So you wanta get some ice cream first?"

"Sure, where are we going?"

"How about my place? Miss Emmaline gave me some leftover strawberries from her jelly making and I made some ice cream this afternoon. You like homemade ice cream?"

"Are you kidding me? I haven't had any in forever. I'd love some."

Hearing that, Cameron turned the truck around and headed back away from town and toward Grey's Station. A few minutes later, he pulled the truck around to the back of the house and reached across Peyton to open the door for her.

"Thank you, kind sir," she said in surprise.

Cameron tossed her the keys and said, "I'll be right in. I have to get the baby monitor. It needs new batteries. Make yourself at home."

Peyton stepped out of the truck and walked the few steps to the porch and turned to look at Cameron. He was collecting a toolbox from the truck bed and smiled back at her. She gave him a little wave with two fingers, then unlocked the back door and went inside.

Walking briskly out to the barn, Cameron opened the wooden door and looked inside. Even though it was twilight outside, the barn's interior was pitch dark. Reaching for the hanging chain to turn on the light, Cameron felt a sudden dull thunk on the back of his skull. The toolbox fell from his hand hitting the ground and opening, scattering hammers, wrenches, and screwdrivers everywhere. A sky full of stars presented themselves before his eyes just as he fell to the ground with a thud. Someone slid the barn door closed. Suddenly the barn was dark again.

Chapter Twenty:
Cameron is Hurt

PEYTON BUSIED HERSELF LOOKING AROUND THE SMALL, slightly untidy kitchen while she waited for Cameron to return. The refrigerator was covered with pictures of Ruthie. In the upper right hand corner was a family portrait of the three of them – Cameron, Jane and Ruthie - that brought a tear to Peyton's eyes. She decided to wash the dishes that were in the sink. Putting the stopper in and pouring a drop of dishwashing detergent into the sink, she ran warm water to cover the dishes. She looked in a drawer near the sink and found a stack of dishcloths, neatly folded.

These were Jane's, she thought. *Poor girl. Life truly wasn't fair.* She washed the dishes – a collection of cereal bowls, spoons, coffee cups and sippee cups – and stacked them neatly in the dish drainer. She walked to the living room and looked at the books and family photos lining the shelves of the bookcase. Picking up a photo of Ruthie turning a lopsided cartwheel, she smiled involuntarily. She looked at her watch and realized she'd been in the house alone for fifteen minutes.

Where can he be? Working on his tractor again, she thought. She went to the back door, called Cameron's name, and waited. Nothing.

She skipped down the steps and walked quickly to the barn. Sliding open the door, she waited for a moment for her eyes to adjust to the darkness. She reached for the light chain and pulled it on.

"Cameron?"

Silence. A faint movement drew her eyes to the ground next to the tractor and she looked down.

Her hand went involuntarily to her mouth and she suppressed a scream. There, lying on the earthen floor of the barn was Cameron. A tiny pool of blood had formed beneath his head and he moaned softly. She dropped to her knees and put her hand on Cameron's shoulder.

"Cameron!" she called and caressed his chin with her hand. "Are you ok? Cameron? What happened?"

Cameron groaned, opened his eyes slowly and put his hand to the back of his head. Wincing when he found the spot where he'd been hit, he muttered, "Did you see him? Where'd he go?"

He pulled his hand back and saw the blood that had come from his wound.

"Where'd who go? What happened?"

"I just cut on the light and somebody hit me over the head. That's all I know. Did you see anybody?"

Cameron sat up gently and rubbed the back of his head where a goose egg was beginning to form. He put his hand on the tractor wheel and pulled himself up. Peyton put her arm around his waist and helped to lift him.

"Be careful, Cameron. Are you sure you should be moving around? Maybe we should get you to a doctor."

"Nahh, I'm ok, I just got the breath knocked out of me. I just can't figure out what happened.

"OK, let's go inside but I'm sticking with you for a while till you're sure you're ok."

Peyton put her arm around Cameron's waist and steadied him as they walked slowly toward the house. He kept his hand over the back of his head as though sheltering it from another blow. Entering the kitchen, Peyton drew up a chair and helped Cameron into it. He touched the back of his head softly and winced.

"Ouch, that really hurts! Get me the ice pack that's in the freezer, will ya?"

"So quit touching it already. I still think we should get you to a doctor."

Peyton wrapped the ice pack in a kitchen towel she'd retrieved from a drawer and handed it to him. Cameron silently formed the word "no" and placed the ice pack that Peyton handed to him onto the back of his neck. The bleeding had stopped and the swelling was beginning to subside.

"Cameron, seriously, I'm scared. Who would have done this? We should definitely take a pass on the fireworks. I think you've already seen enough stars for one night. That ok with you?"

"Yeah, you're probably right. I'm just glad Ruthie wasn't here. I may call my sister and tell her to keep her another couple of days while I find out what's going on around here."

"That's not a bad idea. Shouldn't we call someone? What can I do to help?"

"Right now, just come with me over to the sofa and let's sit for a little bit while my head gets straight." He kept the ice pack resting gently on his wound.

Peyton walked beside Cameron slowly, holding on to him carefully as he eased himself down onto the sofa cushion. She positioned herself at the other end of the sofa.

JANET MORRIS BELVIN

"Hey, what's with the long distance? I'm positive I'll heal faster if you're closer."

Peyton moved gently near Cameron and tucked herself under his shoulder.

"Are you sure this is ok?"

"Look at me. See, I'm feeling better already."

"Seriously, Cameron, this is scary. Why would anyone be hiding in your barn? What were they doing out there? Do you think we should call Barry?"

Barry was Barry James, the sheriff of Braverton Mill. A man of about 50, he had served the community faithfully and well for nearly half his life.

"Yeah, I'll call him now but don't know if he'll come out here. Sheriff's probably got his hands full at the fireworks right now. You know that reminds me of something. He came around here the other morning while you were in town. Said he had been talking to a couple more of the local farmers around here who reported some missing farm chemicals from their barns. Said we should keep a watch out for anyone suspicious around the barns at Greyson."

"Do you think whoever did this might have been in your barn looking for chemicals? What would they want them for anyway?"

"They use some farm chemicals to make explosives or in meth labs – you know, drug labs to make methamphetamines. They steal anhydrous ammonia from tanks temporarily parked on farms. So far, I haven't seen any evidence of any of that but I haven't checked the barns down at The Refuge. I'll do that tomorrow afternoon after my head clears up a little."

Cameron pulled his cellphone from his jeans pocket and punched in the 911 code. The dispatcher answered instantly and Cameron told her about his attack. Peyton watched his face constantly for any signs of further distress or pain. Told by the dispatcher that a deputy unit would be there right away, Cameron thanked her and shut off his phone.

"So what did they say?" Peyton asked. "Are they coming right over?"

"Yes, but right now, I think I need a little time with my nurse. Could you check to see if she's on call?"

Cameron pulled Peyton closer to him on the sofa, and pushed off the boot from one of his feet with his other foot. Then he reversed the process and put his feet up on the table in front of the sofa.

"Now, come here, you," he said and turned his head to kiss her. "Ow!"

Peyton sat up with a start and said, "Oh, my gosh, I'm sorry. What'd I do?"

"Nothing. I just turned too quickly. I think I'll feel better if you kiss me right here," he said, pointing to the corner of his lips. "Now here," and he pointed to the other side. "See? I'm already feeling better. I think you better stay with me, though, just in case I take a turn for the worse."

"I was just thinking the same thing," Peyton replied softly and nuzzled under his outstretched arm.

Within minutes the deputy sheriff's car pulled into the driveway at Grey's Station and Sheriff Barry James emerged from the car. He looked around the yard, walked purposefully up to the porch and knocked. Peyton got up and let him in.

"Hey Sheriff. Cameron's in the living room. Somebody hit him pretty hard out there in the barn."

He threw up his hand in greeting when he saw Cameron. The sheriff pulled a straight chair next to Cameron and proceeded to pull a notebook and pen from his back pocket.

"Thanks for coming, Barry," Cameron began. "I thought you'd be too busy with the fireworks tonight."

"No worries, man. I've got two deputies there and we're covered. Now, tell me. Did you have anything missing?"

"Well, to be honest, I haven't had a chance to look, but I don't think so. I didn't have much stored in that barn except my tractor and a few tools."

"I wonder if maybe the attack isn't related somehow to the theft of farm chemicals farmers have been experiencing in the county," Barry asked. "We've been watching the farms in the county for any suspicious activity. But there are just too many farms and not enough deputies."

Peyton told him about Taylor's shady demeanor in the bank. Barry replied that "he'd been contacted by the SBI who'd asked him to monitor the banker's actions. There'd been some irregularities in the bank's accounting as bank examiners had discovered.

"The bank's Board of Directors alerted the SBI who contacted me to be watching," Barry noted. "How brave do you feel, Peyton? I think we could nab ole Taylor in a sting if you've got the nerve."

Peyton looked nervously at Cameron and then back to Barry.

"If it means we can catch Taylor at his tricks, I'm in."

"Now hold on, Peyton. I'm not sure it's a good idea for you to get involved. If the SBI is watching this, you could be in real danger," Cameron cautioned.

Peyton shook her head and looked down. She waited a moment before responding, then said, "You know, Cam, this property has been in my family for decades. My Mama and Daddy worked hard to maintain it, just as I know you have. I'm not about to let Taylor or whoever is lurking around take away everything my family built."

"OK, the sheriff replied. "It means you're going to have to play along with whatever Taylor suggests. If he wants you to sell some land, be agreeable. Don't sign anything, of course, but you've got to seem to agree with him. I think he's got more on his mind than just those trees and land of yours. I'm not at liberty to say just yet. But we've had our eyes on him for a while.

He's been hanging out with some questionable characters lately. I'll fill you in when I know more.

"Be on the lookout for anyone you don't recognize around here asking questions, anybody who looks like they don't belong, anyone with odd behavior. Make a note of their physical characteristics – height, weight, tattoos, piercings and so on. And look out for any unfamiliar vehicles. Try to get the vehicle make, model, color, any bumper stickers or body damage. And a license plate number would be extremely helpful."

"Thanks, Barry. 'Scuse me if I don't get up," Cameron grinned.

With that, Barry settled his hat on his head and took his leave, reminding Peyton to look after Cameron and watch her back. Peyton walked him to the door and thanked him. Locking the door, she walked back to Cameron.

"I'm so glad Ruthie is staying with Sue and Charlie for a bit," Cameron said, his face still a bit pale.

"I know. Let's hope we can get all this cleared up sooner rather than later. Now I'm going to get you a fresh ice pack. So you just sit tight. I'll be right back."

Chapter Twenty-One:

A Discovery

THE NEXT MORNING CAMERON OPENED HIS EYES AND REACHED his hand to the back of his head. It was still hurting but less than the day before and the swelling was down, a good sign in his opinion. Peyton had stayed late, calling his sister Sue to fill her in on the details of Cameron's assault and then fixing a supper of soup and grilled cheese sandwiches for them both. For the rest of the evening, they had sat on the sofa, looking at old photos and yearbooks. Around 11:00, Peyton had taken Cameron's keys and driven herself back to Greyson, promising to bring back the truck first thing in the morning. Cameron had protested, insisting he was ok to drive her home, but Peyton prevailed and had called him ten minutes later to let him know she'd gotten in safely.

He got up slowly from the bed and drew the covers up loosely, then walked to the bathroom. He turned the shower on full blast. Steam began to rise from the floor of the shower and Cameron dropped his boxers to the floor. He eased his body under the shower's flow, taking special care around the place on his head where he'd been hit. He tenderly massaged his scalp with shampoo, and then rinsed the dried blood and soap from his hair. He reached for the bar of soap from the soap holder on the tile shower wall and brought it to his nose, reveling in the clean scent. Then he soaped and rinsed his face, his well-muscled arms and the taut muscles of his torso, and finally his long legs. With just a few moments of standing under the water's stream, he was ready to emerge, a new man.

He was standing barefoot and zipping up his khakis when he heard a knock on the back door. Toweling his wet hair carefully so as to avoid the tender spot, he went to the kitchen to answer the knock. A big smile broke out on his face when he saw it was Peyton.

"Hey, early bird! Whatcha got in the bag?"

Peyton came in carrying a brown paper grocery bag and set it on the kitchen counter, along with Cameron's keys and her wallet.

"Breakfast, like I promised. I stopped by the café. How's your head this morning?"

"It's better. I took some aspirin and slept like a baby. I'm hungry this morning so that's a good sign I'm fully recovered! Let me help you get that all set up."

"Hey, back off. I'm still not convinced you're fully recovered. You got an apron around here?"

Cameron pulled a frilly calico apron from a bottom drawer and Peyton was momentarily taken aback. It had obviously been Jane's. She couldn't say anything and continued to stare at the piece of cotton as though it might get up and talk. Wordlessly, Cameron took her shoulders in his big hands and pulled her to him. He wrapped her in an embrace so tender that she seemed to melt in his arms. She rested her cheek on the triangle of silky hair on Cameron's chest and closed her eyes, breathing in his clean, fresh scent. Then, wordlessly, he withdrew from her, turned her around and proceeded to tie the apron on her.

"Jane wouldn't want me to be alone," he said with just a tiny note of sadness in his voice. "Don't ever think she would. So no more worries – ok?"

Her confidence somewhat restored, Peyton nodded and set to work. Cameron walked over to the dryer in the laundry room and pulled a clean grey tee shirt out. Pulling it over his head, he winced slightly as it moved across his wound. Soon Peyton had breakfast on the table. A cheese omelet, strips of crispy bacon and sliced tomatoes soon graced the plates of Cameron and Peyton who sat at the round pine table in the center of the kitchen. A sense of peace surrounded Cameron even as he still felt the knot on the back of his head. *Things just seemed to be better when Peyton was around*, he thought. "Guess what I got in the mail yesterday," Peyton offered, stabbing a piece of her omelet. "A whole sheaf of manuscripts to read for Oxford. Guess they figured I'd had enough time off."

"So when are you gonna start that?"

"Just as soon as I'm sure you're ok and that there are no more bad guys around here."

"Hey, I'm fine. Don't worry about me. In fact, I'm gonna pick up Ruthie tomorrow. Why don't you ride over with me to Fairfax?"

"OK, I'd like to meet your sister anyhow. What time you planning to leave? I was thinking I might run over to the auction at the fairgrounds for a bit later this morning."

"Not sure yet. I'll let you know."

The two finished eating, talking easily for another quarter of an hour, then gathered the dishes into the sink. Peyton washed and Cameron dried and put them away, all the while discussing farm matters and Ruthie's latest saying.

One hour later, after having been driven there by Cameron, Peyton was back at Greyson sitting in a rocker on the back porch. A glass of iced tea sat on a small wicker table beside her chair and in her lap were ten manuscripts to be perused. She sighed periodically and read through page after page, occasionally jotting down notes on a yellow legal pad.

As soon as he dropped off Peyton at Greyson, Cameron slid into his truck and drove the short distance to The Refuge. He'd been planning to take a look at the fields there but something kept telling him all was not right there .He hoped a look around in the daylight might prove he was wrong. Driving through the oak-lined path, Cameron scanned the fields on both sides of the path, noting which seemed accessible to his big machinery. He thought all seemed normal so he decided to take a look at the barns farther back in the woods. The truck bounced along the rutted dirt road for the five minutes it took him to get back into the woods where the two barns were located. As he neared the turn leading into the opening where the barns stood, something seemed amiss. Cameron couldn't quite put his finger on it, but knew somehow that he did not want to be seen. So he pulled the truck into a heavily wooded area and stilled its motor.

Walking silently through the underbrush, he came upon the clearing in front of the barn and spotted an unfamiliar truck there. He pulled back into the underbrush and waited for what seemed an eternity. Crouching behind a group of trees, he listened for a moment and heard noises from the direction of the barn. Finally, two men walked out of the barn, scanning the horizon carefully. One was a tall man with a mustache and several days' growth of beard. The other was a somewhat shorter man dressed in a business suit. His face was hidden by the brim of his panama hat but by his stance and self-assured walk, Cameron recognized him instantly – Taylor Jamison! What was he doing here on Peyton's property?

The pair got into the truck and backed around, then quickly left the barns. Cameron waited a few moments to be sure they weren't returning, then walked up to the barn. The doors were padlocked as he expected, but he was able to separate the doors enough to look through the crack between them. The bright sun was enough to illuminate the barn's interior through the crack. What he saw inside stunned him. A crude table of planks set up on sawhorses stretched across the back of the barn. Underneath were an assortment of mason jars, lithium batteries, chemicals and other drug paraphernalia. Just to the right of the sawhorses, Cameron saw four large farm chemical tanks.

On closer inspection, he noted they were anhydrous ammonia. Nearby were bags of other chemicals Cameron knew to be high risk – ammonium nitrate, potassium nitrate, sodium nitrate. The presence of these chemicals in this amount sent up huge red flares in Cameron's mind.

This stuff shouldn't be here, he thought. *What the... Looks like ole Taylor's got himself a drug lab. Either that or he's making bombs.*

Waiting for a few minutes until he was sure Taylor and his accomplice were gone, Cameron got back into his truck, started the engine and drove slowly back to Grey's Station.

"I've got to tell Peyton," he thought. Then we need to alert Barry."

Chapter Twenty-Two:
The Auction

ABOUT AN HOUR LATER, TAYLOR PULLED HIS CADILLAC INTO an isolated parking spot on the county fairgrounds. *Don't want anybody to scratch the paint on this baby,* he thought to himself.

The parking lot was filled with dozens of cars whose owners were high rollers attending the auction there for one reason – to pick up a young bull for breeding or a sport horse for eventing or racing. Bids at these auctions were generally low but occasionally reached several thousand dollars or more. Although Taylor had no plans to buy a horse that day, he wanted to be seen and in Loudoun County, the horse auction was the best place for that.

Most of the horses there for sale were retired Thoroughbred racehorses, horses that had run for insignificant purses at small racetracks around the country and failed to make an impression on anybody. With a good fifteen or twenty more years of life left in them, they made good riding horses for the little daughters of rich men in the county. Those rich men were there in abundance on this day and Taylor meant to impress them with his presence.

Taylor walked around the perimeter of the buyers gathered for the auction, speaking to first one person, then another, making sure to be seen by as many people as possible. He rolled up his program and swatted away a horsefly that seemed determined to land on his nose. Before long, he saw

Peyton across the way almost hidden from view by a knot of buyers in the center of the grounds.

"Peyton!" he called, waving his program and dashed across to see her.

Oh good Lord, she thought. *What now?*

"Hey, Peyton. How are you on this fine day? There's some good lookin' prospects out here today. You're not thinking of picking up another horse, are you? Haven't you already got too much on your plate as it is?"

"Oh, hey, Taylor. I'm just having a look around. I may pick up something if the mood strikes me. I thought it might be fun to have another horse around in case I want to ride with a friend."

"You mean your hired man, don't you? He's not really your class of folks, is he?"

Peyton stopped in her tracks and just looked hard at Taylor. Her ire was stirred. She thought for a minute before responding.

"You're right, Taylor – he isn't on my level. He's actually much higher – He's had to work hard all his life and had nothing but hard luck and tough times. He put himself through college and he's really made something of himself. My parents really respected and loved him and that's good enough for me. I don't really need your estimation of him to determine whether or not he should be my friend."

With that, she turned on her heel and walked off in the opposite direction, satisfied at finally telling off the ill-mannered banker.

"Now, hold on, honey," Taylor pleaded, rushing to follow her. "I didn't mean anything by that. I'm sure Cameron's a nice enough fellow. He just doesn't have your background, your breeding ..."

Then, remembering Barry's reminder that she should "play along with Taylor for now," she slowed her walk and smiled.

"Sorry, Taylor, I know you're just thinking of me. Guess I'm still upset from losing my folks. It's been good to see you. I've gotta run," she called over her shoulder. "I saw a colt over there I want to take a look at."

With that, Peyton walked quickly away from the banker who threw his program on the ground in disgust. She was headed for the concession area when she ran straight into a tall man wearing a ball cap.

"Ooh, sorry."

"Hey, what's your hurry, Peyton?"

With relief, Peyton realized it was Cameron. He'd just entered the auction area and was looking around when he saw Peyton talking to Taylor. Striding over in her direction, he had momentarily lost sight of her in the crowd when she ran into him. She looked up at him, reassured that she was out of Taylor's range.

"Oh, Cameron, thank goodness it's you. I was just talking to Taylor over there. He is really starting to creep me out."

"Yeah, well. There's good reason for that. We need to talk. Let's go someplace where it's private."

"How about we go over to my place for a late lunch? I just bought some roast beef. I can make us some sandwiches while we talk."

"Sounds good, Peyton. I'll follow you there."

A few minutes later, Peyton and Cameron were standing in the big kitchen at Greyson. Peyton smiled again as she remembered the many times she'd seen her mother standing at this very same granite topped counter making lunches for her father. She imagined her mother in front of the large AGA stove. On the next wall beside the stove, a tall Sub-Zero refrigerator and freezer commanded most of the space. Opposite the stove wall was another counter which had a sink made of soapstone. In the center of the room was an island with four tall stools. The island's surface was of butcher block and contained a small bar sink. A large farm table surrounded by eight Windsor chairs stood near the door leading to the porch. Across the heart pine floors, several small oriental rugs were scattered. The room was warm and inviting and seemed a safe haven to both Peyton and Cameron.

They stood side by side at the island, Cameron thinly slicing the roast beef on a cutting board while Peyton assembled the sandwiches. Plunking them down on her mother's Mottahedah plates, she said,

"I can't believe I ran into Taylor at the auction. Doesn't he ever go to the bank? And what's this big secret you've gotta tell me. I can't wait any longer."

"Sit down, first. And what've you got to drink in that giant refrigerator of yours?"

Peyton stuck out her tongue at Cameron and grabbed two long – neck bottles from the door. She set them on the table along with a plate of chocolate chip cookies she'd thawed out and baked, pulled two blue-checked cloth napkins from a drawer in the island and tossed them toward Cameron. Pulling a chair back from the table, she sat down and looked at Cameron expectantly.

"No," she admitted. "These aren't made from scratch cookies. Cooking is not one of my talents! Well?" she said.

"I think you've got a drug lab on your property."

"A what?"

""Yeah, I was thinking about preparing those fields around The Refuge for planting winter wheat so I decided to take a look and see how bad they were. I'd had a funny feeling about the barns over there ever since we walked through the house. So I drove over there this morning after you left. I saw a truck parked back there that I didn't recognize so I pulled mine over into the trees where it couldn't be seen and waited awhile. Pretty soon ole Taylor and some guy with a three days' growth of beard came walking out of the barn."

"What the heck were they doing in MY BARN?" Peyton practically shrieked.

"I'm getting to that. I waited till they left. I'm pretty sure they didn't see my truck or me. After a while I looked into the barn and saw it was full of chemicals, containers and other stuff that I guess you'd use to make methamphetamines or explosives or something. The county extension agent had a course a few months ago for local farmers on how to prevent that from happening at your farm. I had been meaning to talk to Mr. Jimmy about it and then the accident happened. Things have been pretty crazy around here since then. I blame myself, really."

"Don't be silly, Cameron. There's nothing you could have done. I've always felt weird around Taylor Jamison anyhow. I'm not surprised. So you think Taylor's involved in drugs somehow? What should we do now?"

"Well, the county agent said we should upgrade the lighting and lock up chemicals but those chemicals out at The Refuge didn't come from Greyson. I keep any we use under lock and key in a storage room in the big white barn. There's just too much of the stuff out there at the Refuge. They've obviously been hauled in here from somewhere else. Taylor's probably been watching for just such a place as this. The Refuge has been abandoned for so long. And with your parents gone, he figured it would be the last place we'd be working for the next few months. Perfect place to make a little cash."

"So what do we do now? We need to contact the sheriff?"

"Yeah, I've already done that – but I think we're going to need to set up a little sting operation – you know, catch Taylor in the act, so to speak. Whatdya think?"

"I'm in. What do we do first?

"Well, nothing right now – The sheriff's working on a plan but it is probably gonna involve the two of us. You think you're brave enough?

"Are you kidding? Nothing would make me happier than to take that pompous ass down a few pegs. Let's get going."

"Now, hold on. We've got to keep from arousing his suspicion, especially since I was down at the barn this morning. We've got to act like everything's normal. So I'm gonna spray that field of beans up near the main house. You probably oughta go do some work yourself. Weren't you planning to paint that little dairy house in the back yard? "

"Yeah, I was. It just seems that waiting is gonna give them a chance to get away with something."

"Don't worry. The sheriff's gonna call me in a couple of hours with his plan. I'll let you know the minute I hear something. Whatdya say we run over to Fairfax this afternoon and see Ruthie. I might just get my sister to keep her another couple of days, just to be on the safe side."

"Yeah, that's probably a good idea. What time you want to go over there?"

"Well, she usually has dinner ready by six. Want me to pick you up around five? I'll let her know to set another couple of places for us. I told you she's the world's best cook, didn't I?"

"Yeah, you mentioned that," Peyton said dryly and swatted him with her napkin.

Chapter Twenty-Three:
A Visit with Sue and Charlie

At 5:00 on the dot, Peyton climbed up into the cab of Cameron's Ford truck and settled herself. Buckling her seatbelt, she looked out the window at Maudie and Skipper, grazing contentedly.

"You know I need to start riding Maudie more. "I was thinking of buying another horse. If I did, would you consider riding with me? I saw a real nice looking bay at the preview for the auction the other day. A fellow from near Round Hill brought him in to sell. I don't think he ever got sold but I got his number. We could go out some time and take a look."

"Sure. I'm probably not as good a rider as you but I'm game! Let's get this Taylor mess cleared up and then we'll see what we can find."

"OK – you know the annual August horse show and sale takes place in a couple of weeks. If the bay doesn't work out, maybe we can find something else then."

Cameron turned the truck around on the gravel driveway, and then headed out toward Fairfax. The highway passed farm after farm of beautiful pastures containing stone barns and herds of cattle or horses. It was restful to Peyton just to look at it all, so it was a fairly quiet ride. Peyton asked Cameron to tell her more about his childhood. He'd grown up on a farm near Leesburg but he and his sister entered the foster care system at fourteen when his parents died, his father with a heart attack at age 50 and his mother a year later from cancer. Then they'd lived in three or four foster homes until aging out at eighteen. Sue left the system a year later. With the help of the Boys' and Girls' Clubs of Leesburg, the Hill siblings had been able to stay in school. Cameron entered Virginia Tech's Agricultural Management program on a full scholarship, graduating right on time several years later. That's when he got a job as a farm manager at Greyson. Sue entered George Mason University as soon as she graduated from high school. She met Charlie there in her sophomore year.

An hour later Cameron and Peyton were pulling into the driveway in Fairfax of a small gray cottage trimmed in white. The door was painted a bright yellow. On either side of the door were golden Aucuba bushes. Planted in the flower beds in the front of the house were yellow miniature marigolds.

"Oh, Cameron," sighed Peyton. It's so adorable it just takes my breath away. How long have Sue and Charlie lived here?"

"They built this house right after they found out they were pregnant with the twins. It's hard to believe they've been here for about five years."

"Ruthie must love coming over here. Oh look, they've got such a cool playhouse in the back."

"Yeah, Charlie built it a couple of years ago when the twins were old enough to start playing outside. He's pretty handy with tools. I think doing carpentry work takes his mind off all the stuff he deals with as a lawyer."

"How did Charlie and Sue meet?"

"They ran into each other, literally. They were walking down the street in college talking to friends and not watching where they were going, so Charlie bumps into Sue. He's carrying a Coke in his hand and he spills it all over the front of Sue's tee shirt. Well, it was Sue's brand new tee shirt so she was pretty upset. Charlie offered to buy her a new one and when she wouldn't let him, he said 'can I at least buy you dinner?' Then he smiled at her and she fell for him. I always told her she was easy!"

"Oh, Cameron, what a cute way to meet. I wonder…"

At just that moment, the yellow front door burst open and two blonde whirling dervishes rammed into Cameron's midsection. They were his twin nephews. "Hey, Uncle Cam!" they yelled in unison.

"Hey, losers," Cameron yelled and picked them both up around the midsection. "Oh Peyton," he said in a fake serious voice. "Looks like Sue forgot to take out the trash. I'm gonna just put these in the can for her and then I'll be right in."

"Wait…wait," the two boys yelled, giggling. "It's us, Uncle Cameron."

"Oh, sorry, boys, guess I made a mistake," Cameron grinned. He set the boys down and ruffled the tow-headed twins' hair. "Hey, where's your cousin?"

A tall woman with short brunette hair walked up to the open door, her apron stained with chocolate. She smiled at the commotion outside her front door.

"Me, Daddy, me," Ruthie said. She was perched squarely on Sue's hip and had a definite ring of chocolate around her mouth.

"Hello, you old reprobate," Sue said and hugged her brother with one hand while holding onto her niece with the other. "Ruthie and I have been frosting a cake for dinner. This has gotta be Peyton. Wow, Cameron, you're kinda outa your league here, aren't you?"

"She's funny, isn't she? A real barrel of laughs," Cameron said to Peyton, deadpan. "What's for dinner?"

"Hey Peyton. Nice to finally meet you. Come on in, you two," Sue answered with a smile and another hug for her brother. "I've got a vegetable dinner. Charlie's been harvesting from the garden so fast I can't keep it all cooked up."

"Sounds good, kiddo. Let's get these little knotheads washed up. I'm starved," Cameron said and picked up the twins again. He carried them through the living room into the kitchen where he proceeded to wash their hands at the kitchen sink.

"Peyton, this is Will and this is Noah, otherwise known as the 'Terrible Twosome.' Boys, this is Miss Peyton Thurman. She's a real good friend of mine so be on your best behavior and she might get to be your friend too."

"I'd like that, boys. How old are you?"

"Five," shouted Will.

"Four and three – quarters, Will," Noah yelled back.

"How old are you, Peyton?" Will said, squirming to get away from his uncle's washcloth.

"Old enough!" Peyton answered brightly.

Meanwhile Ruthie had come toddling up to her father and lifted her arms to be picked up. She nuzzled her tiny face into his neck and closed her eyes. For a moment, Cameron was still and stroked her silky hair.

"Are you having a good time with your cousins, sweet girl?"

"Wanna go home wif you and Peyton," she replied and nuzzled even further into his neck.

Peyton's heart did a little flip flop in her chest at hearing those words. She reached out and touched Ruthie's cheek. When she did, Ruthie reached her arms out to Peyton to be held and Peyton eagerly took her in her arms. Cameron looked down at the two of them and smiled. He gave Peyton a quick wink, and then turned to get the twins in their booster seats. Peyton settled Ruthie in the high chair and fastened a bib around her neck.

Dinner was fast and loud and exceptionally good. Sue was as good a cook as Cameron had said. Peyton thought with embarrassment of the sandwich meals she had served Cameron in her grand kitchen while Sue had whipped up this masterpiece in her small cottage home.

"I was going to ask you all over to Greyson for a meal, but now, I'm not sure I want to. I'd never be able to come up to your standards, Sue," Peyton confessed.

"You don't actually think she cooks like this every night, do you?" Charlie guffawed. A solidly built man, Charlie had a permanent smile and beautiful head of prematurely grey hair. Sue smacked him with a dishtowel, then wrapped her arms around him for a hug.

Charlie and Cameron cleared the table of their dinner dishes. Peyton offered to help but Sue insisted that she was a first time guest and wouldn't be allowed to do any work.

"Look out next time, though, Peyton," Cameron warned. "Next time we come over, she'll have you scrubbing toilets."

Rolling her eyes at her brother, Sue served thick slabs of chocolate cake with coffee for the adults and a second glass of milk for the children. Everybody agreed that it was the perfect finish to her delicious meal. and grinned. "Let's go out on the deck. I think it's cool enough."

Charlie and Sue's deck overlooked a large expanse of lawn that was not visible from the front of the house. In the twilight, thousands of lightning bugs were skimming the grass and floating toward the sky. Will and Noah, followed by Ruthie, chased after them. Will found a Mason jar whose lid had been punctured by a nail, obviously prepared ahead of time for just such an activity. Noah stuffed some grass inside and set it down by his mother. For the next half hour, Cameron and Peyton, Sue and Charlie watched with delight as the three children chased the bugs all over the yard, never once succeeding in catching one.

When the lightning bugs finally disappeared and the moon came out, the children settled by their parents. Ruthie crawled up into Cameron's lap and proceeded to fall asleep.

"Lemme just put her to bed. She's been playing hard all day with the boys," said Sue.

"I'd like to take her home tonight," Cameron said, "but I think maybe she better stay here for a coupla days if that's ok. There's something going on over at Greyson that we can talk about when we get the kids down for the night."

He kissed her cheek and handed her to Sue who took her inside. Charlie gathered the boys and marched them to the bathroom where he ran a tub of water and plopped them in.

When they were alone on the deck, Cameron leaned over to Peyton beside him and kissed her nose. "Having fun?" he said.

"I love your family," Peyton replied a bit wistfully. "I always wanted a brother or sister."

"Maybe there's a way we can make that happen sometime. You can borrow mine! But right now, we better get you back home since Ruthie's spending the night here again."

After Ruthie was tucked in and the twins were bathed and put to bed, Sue and Charlie came back out on the deck and sat down to talk. Peyton and Cameron told them about the discovery of the chemicals in the Refuge barn and about Taylor's attempt to purchase property from Peyton.

Sue was immediately concerned for Peyton's safety and asked if she didn't want to stay there in Fairfax with her and Charlie until the police could resolve the problem. Peyton refused graciously and said she needed to be at Greyson to watch over things.

"Cameron, you better make sure Peyton stays safe, you hear? And I'm keeping Ruthie until I hear the situation has been taken care of."

"Call us when you learn anything," Charlie said.

"Thanks, you two. I appreciate that and I'm taking you up on your offer. I'll look after Peyton for sure."

The two couples sat in the back yard until the moths began to bother them so they went inside. They walked into the living room and hugged goodbye. There were promises to bring the boys over to Greyson and a couple of last digs from Sue to her brother, followed by a tender hug.

"Watch your back, Cam," Sue said with a slightly worried look on her face. "I don't like the sound of that banker you told me about."

"Don't worry about me. I'll be fine. I'll be by to pick up Ruthie in a couple of days," Cameron said and put his arm around Peyton's shoulder.

They walked out to the truck and stopped by the passenger door. Peyton wrapped her arms around Cameron's broad shoulders and looked up at him with a slow smile.

"I can't remember when I've had such a nice time," she said.

"Even with all your big shot life style in London?"

"Especially with all that. Let's do it again sometime. Soon."

""It's a deal, Cameron said and sealed it with a kiss, right there in the driveway. "Of course you know Sue's watching all this from inside, don't you?" Cameron whispered. Then he yelled to the yellow front door, "Good night, Sue!"

"'Night, Cameron," Sue yelled as Charlie whistled a loud wolf whistle.

Peyton felt her face go bright red. They got in the cab and buckled up for the ride home. Cameron looked over at Peyton and squeezed her knee.

"You know, while you were out there chasing lightning bugs with Ruthie, I got a call from Barry over at the sheriff's office. He's got a plan and I'm not sure you're gonna like it.

"Why wouldn't I like it?"

"They want you to offer to sell the Refuge to Taylor."

Chapter Twenty-Four:
Making Plans

IN THE DEN OF HIS CONTEMPORARY HOME, TAYLOR JAMISON paced back and forth across the maroon and navy Oriental rug. He pulled his hand across his face and yanked a silk pocket square from his back pants pocket to wipe his brow. More sweat beads rolled down from his slightly receding hairline as he continued to mop them.

He listened intently to his caller, then shouted, "OK, Carlos, this is the last pick-up. I want out. You better be loading the chemicals tonight so make sure you've got the cash. Now don't call me at this number again. I thought I made that clear to you!"

He stalked into the kitchen and poured a glass of water from the pitcher in the refrigerator. Reaching into his shirt pocket, he withdrew two little pills and washed them down. *This business is gonna give me a heart attack!* he told himself.

Stabbing at his cell phone with his index finger to shut it off, he looked out the large plate glass window to the mountains beyond and began to formulate a plan. There had to be some way to keep Peyton out of the way of the chemical pick-up that night. Having her walk in on it would be disastrous. Opening the phone once more, he scrolled through the list of contacts, selected her home phone at Greyson and punched in her number.

Meanwhile at Greyson, Peyton closed the back door and leaned against it dreamily. Half afraid to let herself feel what she knew she was feeling, she waltzed over to the sink and began filling it with hot water. Pouring in a little dishwashing detergent, she grabbed a blue striped dishcloth from the drawer beside the sink and began washing the dishes from her breakfast and lunch. She'd been out for a ride on Maude after lunch and left the dishes soaking. She was reliving the kiss at Charlie and Sue's house when suddenly, her reverie was interrupted by the jangle of her mother's black wall phone. Peyton smiled to herself as she crossed the room to pick up the receiver. She'd made fun of her mother so often for not upgrading her kitchen phone to a newer model with caller ID. Now, seeing the old black plastic wall phone gave her a sweet feeling, almost a connection to her mother again. It rang again.

I don't want to seem too anxious. It's probably Cameron, she thought as she put the earpiece to her ear.

"Hello?"

"Peyton, Sweetie? It's Taylor. How you doing this afternoon? "

Oh crap, Peyton thought. *That's why you need caller ID, Peyton!*

"I'm good," she said warily. She was trying to remember exactly what Cameron had told her about the sheriff's plan but all she could recall was something about selling the Refuge.

"Peyton, I want to buy a horse for this lady I've been dating, kind of a pre-engagement gift. Do you know Loretta Gurney? She runs a few hundred head of Red Angus over near Leesburg. She and I have been dating a while and it's getting pretty serious. I don't know a whole lot about picking a good horse and I was wondering if you'd be kind enough to ride with me to look at a little sorrel over at Buck Talbott's place. "

A red flag immediately went up in Peyton's mind since she knew that, as a banker in a rural area, Taylor had to keep up with local livestock owners and their properties. He should be able to assess a horse himself. Nevertheless, she knew she had to play along.

"Why, of course, Taylor. I'll help as much as I can. I'm no expert though."

"But your Mama gave you all those riding lessons so you'll know more than I do. How 'bout if I pick you up in a half hour or so?"

"Make it forty-five minutes to give me time to change clothes."

"OK see you then."

Peyton hung up the phone and immediately called Cameron's number but there was no answer. She tried again two more times but to no avail so she left a message telling him what she was doing. She remembered then that Cameron was discing up a field behind Grey's Station and sometimes he couldn't hear his cell phone over the tractor's engine noise. He probably wouldn't be home until suppertime. Ruthie was still with Charlie and Sue, thank goodness.

Meanwhile, Taylor texted Carlos giving him new instructions for the afternoon. Putting away his phone, he chuckled, congratulating himself on his brilliant idea.

Folding the dishtowel and putting away the dishes, Peyton walked out onto the back porch to see if by chance Cameron had come by. No such luck, so she went upstairs and freshened up.

She pulled a green cotton sweater over her white polo and brushed her hair again. She changed back into her riding boots and jodhpurs and walked back downstairs, planning her demeanor for when Taylor arrived.

While she was on the back porch, she heard the front doorbell's chime and went to open the door. There Taylor stood in what he must have thought were riding clothes – a pair of pressed Ralph Lauren jeans, alligator cowboy boots and a blue Izod sweater tied loosely atop his white polo shirt.

"Hey Peyton, don't you look fresh as a daisy? I really appreciate you helping me out like this."

"I don't know how much help I'll be, but you know women always like to give an opinion," Peyton replied and looked up at Taylor charmingly.

Taylor had brought another one of his vehicles, a huge black Ford F-250, loaded with chrome. Peyton locked the front door behind her and headed toward the truck. Taylor walked Peyton around to the passenger side, his hand lightly on her back. Trying not to shudder, Peyton commented on how nice and clean the truck was.

"I never drive a dirty vehicle. It reflects badly on me."

Oh yes, and you've got quite the reputation to protect, Peyton thought.

They made the thirty minute drive in a little under twenty minutes, thanks to Taylor's radar detector, and soon turned into a long lane marked by a sign reading:

TALBOTT FARM

LEESBURG, VIRGINIA

REGISTERED THOROUGHBREDS

The lane was bordered by a long line of tall oaks on each side and led up to a one and a half storey frame dwelling with a front porch bearing six square columns.

"Now this may not look like much compared to your Greyson," Taylor whispered with a wink," but Mrs. Talbott puts her money where it counts – in her breeding stock – and in my bank!"

They emerged from the truck and walked over to the paddock immediately behind the house. A little woman in dirty jodhpurs, boots and tee shirt, Emily Talbott was leaning against the fence, her right foot resting on the lower fence rail.

"There's Mizz Talbott," Taylor called out, the very image of the good old boy.

"Hey Taylor," Mrs. Talbott called out. "You don't have another girl-friend, do you? I declare they get younger and prettier all the time."

"No ma'am. This is Miss Peyton Thurman, lives up at Greyson. She's the one I was tellin' you about."

"Law child, I heard about the accident. I'm just as sorry as I can be. You know, your mama and I were in high school together. "

Peyton blushed and muttered a quiet thank you. After a moment of uncomfortable silence, Taylor cleared his throat and asked to see the little mare that was for sale. With evident relief, Mrs. Talbott whistled to the sorrel mare cropping grass in the far corner of the paddock and proceeded to show her off.

Taylor pretended to know nothing about horses and relayed every question to Peyton or Emily. After much hemming and hawing during which time Peyton looked repeatedly at her watch, a deal was struck and Taylor shook hands with the owner. He promised to have the animal trailered over to Mrs. Gurney's farm within the week and repay her for feeding the mare until he picked her up.

Getting back in the truck, Taylor suggested a stop at the local Starbucks for a cup of coffee, but Peyton demurred, saying she had a stack of manu-scripts to read. Taylor looked at his expensive Rolex, realized they'd been gone over two hours and said of course he'd take her right home.

Overhead, clouds began to roll in, evidence of an oncoming summer storm so Taylor hustled Peyton into his truck and pushed the ignition. He drove above the speed limit and before long, he was entering the lane to Greyson. Upon seeing the Greyson sign, Peyton felt an inward sigh of relief and braced herself for the hug she knew Taylor would give her. As expected, he reached over to the passenger seat and put his arm around Peyton's shoulder.

"Appreciate the help this afternoon, Peyton. Hey, before I go, are you still seeing Cameron Hill? Folks in town have been talking about you dating the help. Maybe you want to think about that a while."

Taylor gave him a quizzical look, remembered the part she was to play and said, "Don't you worry about me. Glad to be of service today, Taylor. I better get in. It's starting to rain. See you later."

Taylor gunned the engine and raced down the drive, scattering pebbles in his wake. Peyton bounded up the back porch steps and pulled her key ring from the back pocket of her jeans. She prepared to insert the key into the lock, but before she could, the door swung open. It was unlocked!

Chapte Twenty-Five:

The Storm

PEYTON CAREFULLY PUSHED THE HEAVY BACK DOOR OPEN ALL the way and peered inside.

I never leave the house unlocked. What is going on? I know I locked the door when I left with Taylor!

Then she remembered with relief that she'd been on the back porch to look for Cameron before going in to change clothes. She must have hurried inside and forgotten to go back and lock the door behind her. She breathed a sigh of relief and turned to lock the door.

Whew! Thank goodness!

She went to the kitchen to try Cameron's number again. Picking up the receiver, she dialed his number and let it ring several times when she heard a noise in the front of the house. Quietly she replaced the receiver, then went out into the front hall to investigate.

As soon as she entered the hall, she heard a terrific crack of thunder close by. A sudden rain storm darkened the sky. She turned to look out the sidelight by the back door and saw to her horror that a huge limb from one of the oaks nearby had been struck by lightning and had fallen on a fence. Maudie and Skipper were spooked and had retreated to a corner of the paddock. They moved from side to side looking for a way to escape. They squealed in terror, reared, and then stood trembling .

Peyton grabbed a slicker from the hall closet and ran out to comfort the horses. She approached them cautiously, knowing that in their terror, they might act in unexpected ways. She found two peppermint drops in the pocket of the slicker and walked slowly to the horses, talking calmly all the while. Soon the horses settled down and Peyton was able to grab their halters and walk them over to the stable. There she put them into two large box stalls and checked to make sure there was plenty of water and bedding. She tossed in a cup of oats in each feed bin, all the while stroking and talking to the animals. When she felt they were calm enough, she pulled her hood up and ran through the rain the short distance back to the house.

She tossed the slicker into a boot tray on the porch near the back door, and went back into the house. Remembering what she had been attempting to investigate when she heard the limb fall, she walked stealthily toward the front hall. There she discovered the front door was open, rain falling onto the floorboards. She was certain she had locked it when she left. All of a sudden, it was quite clear. She'd had an intruder.

She locked the door again and ran to the kitchen where she found her cellphone and texted Cameron.

CAMERON, CALL ME ASAP. I'VE HAD AN INTRUDER.

Almost as soon as she put her phone down, it rang again. It was Cameron.

"Oh, Cameron, thank goodness. I've been trying to reach you. Someone broke into the house while I was out. I accidentally left the back door unlocked while I went over to Leesburg with Taylor…"

"What the heck were you doing with Taylor?"

"He called and asked me to advise him on a horse he was considering for Mrs. Gurney. He said he was dating her and wanted to do something nice for her. So, since you told me to act natural around him, I told him I'd go with him. While I was gone, someone got inside the house. I was just about to see if anything was missing when I heard one of those big oaks in the back yard get hit by lightning. A huge limb broke off and fell onto a section of fence. I had to catch Maudie and Skipper and stable them. They were pretty frightened."

"Have you checked all over the house yet?"

"No, but.."

Grab your keys and cellphone, get in your truck and lock the doors. I'll be right over."

Peyton did as she was told and got into the truck which was parked under the shed. She sat there shivering while she waited for the familiar sound of Cameron's truck. It soon appeared and she pressed the horn briefly to let him know where she was. She got out of the truck and ran to his side, wrapping her arms around his waist, thankful that the storm had ended.

"Come on, let's get you inside, girl."

The two locked the door behind them and walked all over the house looking for any sign of damage or theft, but they saw none. Going back to the kitchen, Peyton brewed a pot of strong coffee and they sat at the table to plan their next move. Suddenly Peyton's cellphone began to ring. She looked at the caller ID, rolled her eyes and answered the phone. She listened quietly for a minute, mouthing the word 'Taylor' to Cameron.

"Can you hold just a minute, Taylor?" Peyton asked. "My tea pot is about to boil over."

She pressed the hold button on her cellphone and looked nervously at Cameron.

"Just play along." I'm going to take my truck down the lane before he gets here. I don't want him to know I've been here. Call me after he leaves. And DON'T tell him about your intruder. Call me when he's gone," he repeated.

Taking a deep breath, Peyton punched the flash button on her cellphone and answered, masking the fear and revulsion that she felt.

"Hey Taylor, I'm just gonna fix myself a little late supper. What can I do for you?"

"Now, honey, I wanted to apologize for that thing I said to you about Cameron earlier today. You know me. I guess I'm like your daddy. I just don't think anybody's good enough for you."

You weasel, Peyton thought. *You're the farthest thing from my sweet daddy.*

"Oh, don't you worry," she said, sugar practically dripping from her lips. "I know you just have my best interests at heart. Why, I never gave it another thought." She rolled her eyes and gave an involuntary shudder.

"Speaking of that, I thought I'd run back over to Greyson real quick. I want us to take a look at that proposition I was talking about. You've still got the papers, don't you?"

"Now, Taylor, I'm kinda tired. Maybe we could talk about it in the morning."

"Sugar, you're not gonna want to wait when you see the numbers on this deal."

Remembering the plan Cameron had told her about, Peyton finally acquiesced. "OK, gimme a few minutes; then come on over."

Fifteen minutes later, Peyton heard the sound of Taylor's big Cadillac Escalade crunching the gravel on the drive. She grimaced and walked toward the front door to wait. Minutes later, the heavy brass door knocker sounded and Peyton pulled open the door.

As soon as she did, she was assaulted by the overpowering odor of his expensive cologne. He gave her a small hug, his manicured fingers patting her hair. Peyton pulled back and shivered a bit. He gave her a wide toothy grin and unnerved her with his direct, penetrating eyes. She couldn't help but notice a slight line of perspiration on his upper lip.

What does he want now?

"Hello, Sugar. Thank you for seeing me again this late. I just had an update on this offer to come in this evening and I couldn't wait to talk to you about it. There's a time limit on it, though, so I didn't want you to miss out." Taylor invited himself in and walked through the sitting room to the dining room table.

"Yes, I was outside with the horses. Lightning struck one of those big oaks out back and a big limb fell on my fence. .."

"That's too bad," he said distractedly. "Now I had a call from that developer I told you about. They want to put the sweetest little development you've ever seen on some of the back acreage you've got. They want to put up about fifty houses in there. Should make you a real nice profit. I know you're going to be headed back to London before too long, so you don't want to have too much hanging over your head back here, now do you? If you do this, we can refinance your loan on your mama and daddy's farm at a real low interest rate and in a coupla years you'll be free and clear. What do you think of that?"

It just grated on her ears to hear all the plans that Taylor had for her land. Thank goodness he didn't know that she was aware of his deception. How much of the profit of this deal would go to Taylor, she wondered. How many details were hidden from her? Peyton remembered standing in the yard of the Refuge with Cameron and looking at the magnificent oak trees lined up one after another, trees that had stood sentry there for hundreds of years. How many of those would be gone if this plan went through?

Taylor tossed a black leather folder he carried under his arm onto the polished surface of the dining room table and pulled out a sheaf of papers with the words "Greyson Housing Development" emblazoned in heavy black type across the top.

Get that mess off my mama's table, Peyton thought, remembering the many times she had seen her mother rub the table carefully with lemon oil.

Taylor fanned the papers out on the table before Peyton and looked at her brightly. Running his fingers through his perfectly combed hair, he cleared his throat.

"Now Peyton, if you'll just take a look at this, the company is offering you a half a million for the property. That kind of money is unheard of in this economy. Just imagine how much fun a single gal like you could have on that kind of a bankroll."

"And what exactly would I be selling?"

"Just those fifty acres back by the river. Your daddy never did farm those. It's just worthless land."

Knowing what she had to do, Peyton forced a smile and agreed to the deal. "Of course I'll have to get my lawyer to go over the papers tomorrow, but I'm sure it'll be ok."

"Why, of course it will, Sugar. I'll just need your signature right here. It's just a paper signifying your intent to sell, that's all," Taylor said, shoving the paper under her hand. "See you at the bank tomorrow morning?"

"OK – how does 9:00 sound?"

"Suits me right down to the ground," Taylor chirped. "See you then."

He gathered up his papers and fairly skipped out the door and down the stairs toward his car. Peyton shut and locked the door and felt again, an uncontrollable urge to wash. Instead, she pulled her cell phone out of her jeans pocket and placed a call to Cameron.

"Well, he came over, just like you said he would. He had the nerve to offer me a half a million for the land where the Refuge is. Said the "developers" were going to put up fifty houses back there.

"Yeah, I think Barry figured him out pretty quickly once I told him what I'd seen out there. Barry says he's involved in a couple of scams – the chemical lab is the big one. I think he wanted to keep the Refuge barn to keep the lab hidden since it's so secluded back there. Selling the oaks would just give him a little play money, " Cameron said, his voice tense and full of portent. "Now you've just got to sit tight and let this thing unfold. I don't think Taylor will wait long to make his next move. Are you ok there by yourself for a bit? Do you want me to come back there? I need to go out and check on the bull pasture. Chairman gets kinda fidgety when we have thunder."

"Don't worry about me. I'm good. Just make sure the Chairman stays in his pen. I wouldn't want to have to deal with that too."

"OK then. Just go on and eat a quick supper and get to bed. I think we've given Taylor enough rope to hang himself. Don't go outside and make sure all the doors and windows are locked. I should have checked all that while I was there. You want me to come up there and do that right now? "

"No, Cameron. Just make sure Chairman is safe. I've got to go out and check on Maudie and Skipper. I want to make sure their stalls are secure."

"NO, Peyton, the horses will be fine. You just need to stay inside. I mean it."

"OK, Cameron. I'll be good. And thank you for being with me in all this mess. See you tomorrow."

Peyton pressed the button to close the call and walked back into the dining room. She moved to the window where, so many decades ago, Thomas Grey had etched his and his bride's name and the date 1723 into the glass. She touched the name with her fingertips, then brought her hand to her heart.

"I can't let this place go," she whispered to no one.

Chapter Twenty-Six:

A Meeting at The Oaks

THE DRIVE BACK TO THE OAKS TOOK TOO LONG, HE THOUGHT. He finally arrived though, and punched in the security code for the gate. Parking the car in one of the four stalls of his garage, Taylor Jamison exited the car, then unlocked the door to the back hall and entered his house. He was nervously pacing back and forth on the expensive Serapi carpet which covered the hardwood floors of his den. He was wishing desperately that he had not stopped smoking cigarettes. He could use one right about now. Taylor was expecting a late night visitor and poured himself a drink to calm his nerves.

That's better.

He ran his fingers through his silvery hair and smiled to himself, recalling how easily he had conned the Thurman girl.

This is literally going to be like taking candy from a baby.

Suddenly he heard a light tap-tap at the back door. He scurried to the kitchen, quickly flipped on and off the outdoor light to see who it was and opened the door.

"Well, get in and be quick about it," Taylor commanded impatiently. "Did you get in?

Carlos Vasquez, Taylor's buyer, sat down imperiously in a kitchen chair. He lit a cigarette and blew out the match, tossing it on the floor.

"Si, I got in. I was able to look around enough to find out what to do with the girl. But you, little man, need to stop ordering me around. My boys and I are the ones doing all the dirty work. Miguel is there right now and he has all the combustibles ready."

"Now, Carlos," Taylor responded nervously, "Back down. I'm sure it's all going to work out. As soon as you torch Greyson and all the fire and police are out there, you can have your trucks back at the old barn in the woods ready to pick up the stuff. Then you can grease my palm and be on your way. No worries, man."

Carlos looked at Taylor with belligerence and shook his head.

I don't trust this old coot, Carlos thought to himself.

"I'm tired of you looking down at me like I'm nothing. This better work or I'll be back – and you'll pay."

He turned on his heel and walked through Taylor's immaculate kitchen, tossed his lit cigarette on the polished wood floor and ground it out with the heel of his scuffed boot. He looked up at Taylor's horrified face and grinned. Then he left, slamming the door behind him.

Chapter Twenty-Seven:

Taken

PEYTON WAS NERVOUS. NOT IN THE MOOD TO PREPARE A BIG meal, she had a bowl of cereal and a glass of orange juice for her supper. She shook her head thinking of how many fine dinners she had enjoyed at that very same table when her mother was alive. *I've got to learn to cook after all this is over*, she thought. She carried her dishes to the sink and made quick work of washing, drying, and putting them away. Thinking it was time to go to bed, Peyton walked to the hall and admired again the magnificent woodwork of the stairway. She put her foot on the first step of the elegant staircase in the front hall when, suddenly, she stopped.

I better take one more check on the horses. Maudie and Skipper were pretty nervous when I fed and watered them this afternoon, she remembered. *I better just go check on them one more time before I go to bed.*

She went through the center hall and scurried out the back door. She grabbed her slicker from the boot tray, and put it on, Standing for a minute on the porch, she surveyed the field behind the house by the light of the moon. Grabbing a couple of sugar cubes from the container on the porch, Peyton descended the steps and walked over to the stable where she'd taken Maudie and her daughter from the pasture. She whistled quietly and the mare and filly came trotting up to their stall doors, whickering softly.

Peyton approached Maudie's box stall leisurely and the mare nuzzled her hand, enjoying the sugar she found there. Peyton rubbed her muzzle and put her head on Maudie's nose for a minute. "OK, old girl. I know you're nervous. Just let me check on the feed room," Peyton said and pulled away from the horse. She gave a sugar cube to the filly in the next stall and gave her nose a rub.

A few feet away from the stalls was a locked room where Jimmy Thurman had kept horse feed and tack for Peyton's two horses. Peyton ambled in that direction. The air was still and quiet with only the occasional sounds of the horses in the nearby stalls.

Suddenly, out of the corner of her eye, she thought she saw a movement outside the stable door and stopped still.

Uh, maybe this wasn't such a good idea, Peyton, she told herself. Then another sudden movement and a flash of white told her it was the retreating rear end of a whitetail deer skipping toward the line of woods in the distance. Two other deer soon followed the first one.

Now settle down, Peyton. You're too jumpy. I'm just going to give the girls a little extra feed tonight.

She lifted the latch on the feed room door and reached inside for the metal bucket her father always kept hanging on the wall. Lifting the lid on the bin nearby, she grabbed the scoop inside and filled the bucket with enough feed for the two horses. She tossed the scoop back inside and closed the bin, then turned and walked back toward the box stalls where Maudie and Skipper waited. Reaching the stall door, she went inside each stall and poured the contents of the bucket in the troughs nearby. She lifted the hose from its hook on the wall, turned on the water and filled the water trough in each stall with fresh water. The horses had ambled up as soon as they heard the clanging of the bucket and began nosing hungrily in their troughs. Peyton gave them a rough pat, and then turned to go back to the shed.

Opening the feed room door, she reached in to find the nail to hang the bucket. At that moment, Peyton heard a noise in the dark corner of the shed. Too late, she looked up and saw a movement inside. She felt a hand grab her wrist and wrestle her to the ground, so suddenly that she had no time to cry out for help. The bucket clattered to the concrete floor with a metallic clang. Shocked speechless, Peyton was conscious only of the smell of sweat and of a dirty rag being stuffed into her mouth. She lay groaning on the shed floor, her eyes wide open, searching for light. Without uttering a word, her assailant had knocked her down, rolled her over and tied her hands behind her back. Peyton groaned and struggled to get free but to no avail. Another loop of rope went around her feet and she was left on the ground while her attacker ran off.

She tried to yell for help, but her voice was muffled by the rag. Slowly, she began to panic. The horses paced back and forth nervously, whinnying. Peyton came to the realization that she was completely helpless. And all alone.

Chapter Twenty-Eight:

Carried Away!

SILENCE. PEYTON WAS AWARE OF COMPLETE SILENCE. THE only sound was the movement of the horses in the stalls nearby as a gentle breeze stirred the trees outside the stable. Terror enveloped her. She was afraid to move for fear of bringing her attacker back. The fear she felt made her tremble. Who knew what he would do to her next? Maybe it was just best to lie still. Maybe he'd think she was dead. But she couldn't be still. Shaking all over, she knew her attacker had been a man but she could tell nothing more about him.

Think, Peyton, think!

In the distance she heard Maudie and Skipper darting back and forth in their stalls, whinnying nervously. What could she do? Suddenly she remembered her cell phone. It was still in her jeans pocket – if she could just wriggle around enough to work it out, maybe she could call for help. She rolled over on the ground and pulled her tied hands together to try to work the phone out of her pants pocket when suddenly, the phone rang!

Oh, God, no. Don't let him come back. I have to get away! I have to get away!

Her heart pounding inside her chest, she wriggled on the floor and felt the phone work its way out of her pocket onto the floor beneath her. She groped frantically with her bound hands behind her to try to find the dial pad. Suddenly Peyton felt herself being grabbed around the middle. She was carried outside the stable and thrown down onto an old tarp on the ground. Hitting the ground with a thud, she heard her attacker pick up her phone from the ground and power it off, then throw it aside. She still couldn't see his face, but from the sweaty smell and his callused hands, she knew he was no one she'd ever seen before. She groaned and pleaded wordlessly for release. Suddenly a metallic clang rang out and Peyton was knocked in the back of the head. Bolts of pain shot through her head radiating from the point of the hit and then everything went black. She was unconscious. Her attacker rolled her in the tarp and picked her up as though she was weightless. He slung her over his shoulders, then carried her away.

Chapter Twenty-Nine:
Checking on the Animals

CAMERON DROVE HIS PICKUP BACK TO THE PASTURES WHERE Chairman grazed. Thurman's Chairman, a Black Angus bull, was normally pretty easy-going. But on nights like this, when lightning flashed across the skies, he was restless, snuffling and pawing the ground around his feet. Cameron walked up to him slowly, talking to him quietly all the time. He checked the gate and inspected all the fencing to make sure it was secure. He patted the bull gently and rubbed the spot behind Chairman's ears, always the best way to calm the giant beast. Finding him relatively calm, he left the pasture, taking care to lock the gate securely and got into his truck.

Driving over to the pasture where Hammer, Jimmy Thurman's prize stallion was kept, Cameron's mind wandered to thoughts of Peyton. He recalled how kind and loving she was to little Ruthie. He remembered the kiss they'd shared at the Refuge and a smile broke across his lips. He recalled how easily she fit into his family at Sue and Charlie's house. Suddenly another crash of thunder echoed outside the cab and Cameron's thoughts came back to the present.

He pulled the truck up outside Hammer's pasture and looked for him without success. Suddenly a brilliant flash of lightening revealed the terrified young stallion running back and forth in a corner of the large paddock where he'd been moved recently.

Frantic when another crash of thunder boomed, Hammer reared, his hooves pawing the sky. Cameron approached him cautiously, cooing and calling the big animal by name. Finally the animal quieted, allowing Cameron to approach him. He laid his hand upon the stallion's quivering withers, whispering his name. He reached in his pocket and found a peppermint candy and held it out for the stallion. Hammer snuffed cautiously, then reached for the candy with his velvety soft lips.

"Attaboy, Hammer. That's the way."

He walked along the fence line, making certain that there were no breaks anywhere. He checked the gate's latch and found it in perfect working order. Finally, assured that Chairman and Hammer were both secured for the night, Cameron got back into his truck and pulled out his cellphone. He turned on the cab light and punched in the number for Peyton's phone, then sat back in the truck while it rang…and rang…and rang.

He hung up and redialed Peyton's number, his nerves building. The call went unanswered again and Cameron shut off the phone angrily. He started the truck, put it in gear and raced toward Greyson…and Peyton.

Chapter Thirty:

Fire!

Everything was black and silent. Peyton sensed nothing. Then slowly from out of a void, she began to regain consciousness. She eased her eyes open and instantly smelled something unusual.

Owww, my head. Where am I? She thought. *And what's that smell?*

Her brain wouldn't focus. She shook her head to clear it, and stopped when the pain returned. Working to align her thinking, she tried to get her bearings. She couldn't see...that much was clear to her. And it began to be clear to her that her airway was severely restricted. Struggling to take a breath, she couldn't remember what had happened to her to put her in this situation. She began reconstructing the night and recalled going out to feed the horses. But that was as much as she could recall. She told herself to focus but she couldn't force her mind to obey. She was only aware that it was hard to breathe and getting harder. There was something about the smell.

That smell...what is that smell?

Suddenly Peyton came to her senses. She remembered what had happened. She'd been feeding the horses and had gone to the shed to return the feed bucket. Someone had bound and gagged her, then hit her over the head. But she couldn't remember who it was who had done this to her...and why. She tried to move but couldn't and came to a horrifying realization.

I must be wrapped up in something because I can't move my arms or legs.

Panic and claustrophobia began to engulf her. She thrashed about on the floor, each movement causing a searing pain in her head. But with the awareness of the ropes around her wrists and ankles came a bleak despair.

An acrid smell persisted and tears came to her eyes. She began to hear a crackling sound and panic overtook her. She tried to yell but the gag in her mouth garbled her voice. She tried spitting out the gag but it was too big. Suddenly she recognized the smell – it was smoke. Something was on fire. Something very near Peyton.

She began rolling over and over. She was inside a building on a hardwood floor. She could tell that much. She rolled again and again but whatever she was rolled in wouldn't unroll. So she rolled herself the other way and miraculously felt her covering begin to loosen. The pain in her head stabbed with each turn yet she knew somehow that she had to continue. She rolled again and again and was able to shrug free of the tarp. But her arms and legs were still bound. She looked down and realized that it had been a dirty old canvas tarp which had imprisoned her. She tried once more to scream but the gag held in place. Her head began to clear a bit and she scanned her surroundings.

Peyton turned her head from side to side but, because of the smoke enveloping her, she could barely see. She could tell she was in a large room somewhere – but where? At each end of the room, she was able to make out large windows – Palladian windows! She must be in the ballroom at Greyson. With renewed strength, she began trying to force the gag from her mouth. She pushed it with her tongue repeatedly until finally she forced it from her mouth.

"Help! Help me," Peyton screamed over and over, ignoring the pain from her head where she'd been hit. "Somebody, help me!"

It was still dark outside. That much Peyton could tell. But an eerie light emanated from one end of the ballroom. And the stench of smoke continued to permeate the air around her face. Fire! The house was on fire and Peyton realized she was unable to get free.

"Oh God, help me!" she yelled. "Fire! The house is on fire. Help me, somebody!"

Peyton continued trying to wriggle free of the ropes which bound her but without success. Suddenly she felt herself being picked up from the floor and slung over someone's shoulder. A very strong man had grabbed her roughly and was moving her. Fear overtook her again. Was this her attacker come back to throw her into the flames?

"Help me. Untie me," she yelled frantically, her head throbbing with each syllable she uttered. But there was no answer. Someone draped a wet cloth over her face and began running. Did her attacker have other, more dreadful plans for her?

Peyton turned her head frantically to get fresh air but the cloth covered her nose and mouth. She had the sensation of descending stairs very rapidly and her head hit twice against a wall. The pain in her head was excruciating. It began to throb even more severely. Still she managed to stay conscious. She knew she had to stay conscious! Someone carried her down another flight of stairs and through a doorway. Her head banged against the door as the man carried her through it. She could tell she had been carried to the outside but by whom? Whoever was carrying her threw her down roughly onto the ground. She could hear the frightened whinnying of Maudie and Skipper in the stable nearby. *I must be outside near the pasture,* she thought. Then someone cut the ropes binding her hands and feet with a pocketknife. She was finally free and she pulled herself slowly to a sitting position, removing the wet cloth from her face, wincing as the pain in her head rolled over her again. She rubbed her wrists and ankles where the ropes had chafed and looked around. It took a moment for her eyes to focus.

"Easy. Take it easy." The voice was Cameron's and she'd never been so glad to hear it.

"Cameron, thank God," Peyton said and threw her arms around his neck. "What happened? Who did this to me? How'd you know where to find me?"

"Take it easy, Peyton. I called you an hour ago but somebody powered off your phone instead of answering it. I figured you wouldn't do that so I knew something was wrong. I called Barry and alerted him. He's got his deputies over at the Refuge right now.

"When I called you and couldn't get an answer, I decided to drive over to Greyson to check on you and when I got here, the place was in flames. I called your name over and over but got no answer. So I just started going all over the house. Finally I found you in the ballroom. Thank God you took me up the back staircase that day or I wouldn't have known the way."

Greyson on fire! It suddenly came into focus just what a close call she'd had. She looked despairingly at her family home.

"But Cameron, who did this to me?"

"I'm afraid I did," a sinister voice answered from out of the shadows. It was Taylor and he bore a large caliber gun pointed straight at Cameron and Peyton. Peyton drew in a breath and clung to Cameron.

"That is, I set the whole thing in motion. My friend Carlos from Mexico or El Salvador or wherever it is he's from – he did the heavy lifting, so to speak. No offense intended, Peyton. Unfortunately, he didn't finish the job, thanks to the big man here."

Taylor waved the gun in Cameron's direction and sneered. "You know, you've always been such a pain, Hill."

"Let her go, Taylor. You can take me but let Peyton go."

"Still trying to play the hero, huh? What good would you do me? You're not the one with the deed, Hill."

A sudden movement behind Taylor took his concentration for a split second, but it was enough to give Cameron a chance to knock the gun from Taylor's hand. Sheriff Barry James and two deputies came rushing up behind Taylor and knocked the banker to the ground. A moment was all it took to have the banker on his stomach with his hands cuffed behind his back.

"Where is this Carlos he's talking about?" Peyton whimpered as Cameron rushed to her side.

"Yeah, we already got a tip that one of Taylor's partners is heading over to the Refuge, I think," the sheriff answered breathlessly. "Name was Carlos Del Villar. He had a drug lab over in Fauquier County and the authorities over there texted me his name. One of his buddies decided to cooperate with the authorities in exchange for a lighter sentence.

"Carlos and a couple of his thugs have been stealing farm chemicals around here for months to make methamphetamines. They were using the old barn over at the Refuge as a holding facility. Taylor knew about this place and set the whole thing up for him. Because of his work at the bank making loans to farmers, he knew the layout of most of the farms around here, so it was pretty easy for him to pinpoint the location of the chemicals on area farms. The Refuge barn had been unused for so long that they thought nobody would suspect it. Lucky for us Cameron spotted them a few days ago and tipped us off."

"But why did Taylor get involved?" Peyton asked, wincing as pain shot through her head.

Taylor was being led over to the sheriff's car. A deputy put his hand on Taylor's head as he entered the back seat so he wouldn't bump his head.

"This is an outrage! You do realize I'm the president of the Bank of Braverton Mill, don't you? You'll hear from my attorney," Taylor yelled as he settled into the back seat of the sheriff's car.

"That's where it gets interesting," Barry smiled. "The bank has been trying to get rid of him for several months. He'd okayed some bad loans and was past retirement age so they've been strong-arming him to retire for a while now. And there was something else going on, too. Apparently, old Taylor liked to play the ponies. Unfortunately, he wasn't very good at it. So he owed a lot of money to some very insistent people and he had been "borrowing" from the bank. The Feds have been watching him for some time now. He had another exit strategy in mind, though. He's been planning to leave the country and just needed enough dough to make it happen. The chemical thefts were only part of it. He was also trying to engineer the sale of the Refuge to a couple of developers who wanted to put about fifty houses back there along the river. He was lined up to receive a pretty sweet commission on the deal if he could have gotten you to sell."

"But how did you find this out?" Peyton asked.

"You know, one of Taylor's thugs, Manuel Cordoba, decided to sing like a bird when I offered him a reduced sentence for information on who was behind it. He told us everything we needed to know. My deputies and I started driving over towards Greyson to talk to you and saw the house was in flames, so we called Cameron. The fool was already on his way over here and ran inside hollering your name, Peyton. We tried to stop him but he wouldn't be stopped."

At the mention of the fire, Peyton turned to look sadly at her parents' home, now smoking and blackened with soot. Three fire trucks and a half dozen firefighters could be seen running about the property making sure the fire was extinguished completely. The deputies were stretching yellow crime scene tape around the shed and yard while a police photographer was snapping photos.

"At least it didn't take out the whole house," she said. "Just that part near my parents' bedroom. I guess I can restore it ...somehow."

"Let's don't worry about that now," Cameron said, wrapping his arms around her. "Come on back to my house for now. We'll deal with all this tomorrow. Is she ok to leave, Barry?"

"Did you get hurt in any way, Peyton?" Barry answered. "Maybe you should get checked out by a doctor first."

The smoke was getting worse and Peyton rubbed her eyes.

"I'll take her by the hospital on our way home, Barry. Call you in the morning? You've got my number if you need anything."

"OK, Cam. But I've already got an ambulance on the way to get Peyton to the hospital. I'm sending one of my deputies over there to take some pictures in case she's more banged up than we think she is. We'll need the photos for evidence. "

"Would everybody please stop talking about me like I'm not here," Peyton interrupted. I can take care of myself!"

She tried to stand but was struck by a sudden attack of dizziness. Cameron strengthened his hold on her shoulders and helped her lie down again.

"Nope! We're going to run by the hospital, Peyton. No arguments. A check-up couldn't hurt."

A wave of nausea swept over Peyton and she swallowed to keep from vomiting. Her head continued to throb and she found her vision was slightly blurred. She looked up gratefully to Cameron and agreed.

"That's probably a good idea, Cam. Not feeling great here."

Chapter Thirty-One:

Rest

AT BARRY AND CAMERON'S INSISTENCE, PEYTON HAD BEEN
seen immediately upon arrival at the hospital. The doctor in attendance,
Dr. Rebecca Livesay, insisted on a rape kit but found no evidence of sex-
ual molestation. She determined that Peyton had nothing more than a few
bruises and lacerations as well as a slight concussion. She gave Peyton a
few stitches in the back of her scalp and ordered a prescription of strong
painkillers for her patient in case the pain became unbearable. But she cautioned Peyton to be careful as they were highly addictive. That was enough
to make Peyton determined to stick to over-the-counter pain relief, if at all
possible. Dr. Livesay was concerned about smoke inhalation so she gave her
an arterial blood gas test, a chest x-ray and a variety of pulmonary function
tests. Finding no evidence of serious, long-lasting damage, she discharged
her patient with a stern warning. Peyton insisted that she felt good enough
to leave the hospital, pledging to return immediately if she got worse. The
doctor recommended ice packs, bed rest, and mild pain relievers, all of which
Cameron was able to supply. He was also to waken her at brief intervals
overnight because of her concussion.

Peyton sat in a wheelchair and a male nurse rolled her out to Cameron's
pickup truck. The nurse and Cameron lifted her gently and helped her to the
passenger seat of the truck cab. Cameron buckled her in, and then drove

slowly to Grey's Station. Peyton drifted in and out of sleep during the ride to Cameron's home.

Several hours later, Peyton was settled in the spare bedroom in Cameron's house. Cameron had called Charlie and Sue to inform them of the evening's events and requested that they not tell the children. They readily agreed and said they'd keep Ruthie until Cameron was ready for her return. Peyton had showered, put on one of Cameron's tee shirts and gone straight to bed. Cameron had wakened her at intervals throughout the night and barely slept himself.

Ten hours later, she awoke. Peyton opened her eyes tentatively and saw Cameron standing in the doorway, eyes focused on her. She tried to sit up but was immediately stopped by the pain in her head and by a reprimand from Cameron.

"Whoa, no sitting up for you right now, young lady. Just relax. Put your head back on that pillow."

"Where's Ruthie?"

"Sue said she'd keep her another day or two. They're going to an amusement park today so she's not even thinking about home right now. She said to tell you she'd see you in a day or so when she brings Ruthie back."

Cameron sat gently on the bedside and took Peyton's hand in his. He closed his eyes for a minute and shook his head, then looked into her eyes. Peyton watched, amazed, as a tear fell from his eye onto the bedspread.

"You know, Peyton, when I lost Jane, I never thought I'd feel love for another woman again. But when I thought I'd lost you in that fire last night, I just about went crazy. I knew if I ever got you back, I'd never want to let you go."

"You saved my life. I don't even know how to respond to that. You could have been killed going all the way up to the ballroom for me. That's three floors. Why did he take me all the way up there anyway?"

"Manuel Cordoba told Barry that Taylor wanted to make sure you couldn't get out. The plan was to defray attention to Greyson so no one would be aware of what's been going on over at the Refuge barns. They planned to load all their chemicals and leave the county while all the attention was focused on the fire at Greyson. So somebody set the fire in the center part of the building after he took you up there. The fire started in your parents' bedroom directly under the ballroom. The front staircase was gone by the time I got there. I was just lucky you'd showed me the back staircase up to the ballroom the other day."

"No, I was lucky. So lucky to have found you."

Cameron leaned down to kiss her forehead. Peyton reached her arms up to Cameron and encircled his neck, sobbing quietly. She put her head on his shoulder and smelled the clean, fresh smell of his shirt. He wrapped his arms around her and held her shoulders in his hands, his face buried deep in her hair.

"You still thinking of going back to your job in London? I'm not sure I could handle that."

"No way, buddy. I'm sticking around here now. I can work from home... if I can get "home" fixed up again. Do you think it's possible? Is Greyson too far gone after the fire? What does it look like out there this morning?"

"It's been badly damaged in that one area but with some repairs, it would be livable again. Now, about what you said about sticking around, are you serious, Peyton?"

"Oh... so serious, Cam. Since being back here, I've come to realize just how much this place is my home. Without my parents, I thought I'd prepare it for sale and go back to London. Now I know I want to stay here...with you and Ruthie if you two want me. I just want you to ask me."

Cameron stood up and paced back and forth beside the bed. "You know you've got bandages all over you and you're pretty banged up. You really aren't at your best right now. You might not even be thinking clearly."

He smiled a lopsided grin and went down on one knee beside the bed.

"Cameron Hill, are you gonna ask me or not?"

"Oh most definitely. I don't deserve you, but I'm gonna ask you."

Chapter Thirty-Two:

A Proposal

PEYTON SAT UP IN BED SLOWLY AND WRAPPED HER ARMS around her knees. A tear leaked from her right eye and she wiped it away. Cameron cleared his throat and looked around the room. He reached for her hand again and enclosed it with both of his larger ones. His eyes looked directly into hers.

"You know, in a way, Peyton, Taylor was right."

"What? What are you talking about?"

"Well, I'm really not in your league. I'm basically just your farm help. You're the owner of this huge operation and you have a terrific job in London with Oxford. Add to that the fact that you're gorgeous, you've got a great education and you could have any man on the planet and, well, it looks pretty ridiculous that I'm down here on my knee asking you to marry me and become a mother for Ruthie."

Peyton looked into his tanned face, the blue eyes so sincere. She put her fingertips on Cameron's mouth to stop him from saying anything else. She smiled sadly and drew him to her breast.

"Cameron, please, don't say that. The way you have taken care of me over these last months has been…well, it has been wonderful. I was sure that I would be lost and lonely for the rest of my life without my parents. And that job in London? I'll either work from here or I'll get another job. I don't ever want to take the chance of living without you and Ruthie for one more day."

A smile broke over Cameron's face. He reached in his shirt pocket and withdrew a gold band with a diamond solitaire, holding it carefully between his thumb and forefinger.

"Oh, Cam…"

"Peyton, I've told you this before, but I have to say it again. When I lost Jane, I thought I would never love again. I pretty much shut myself off from the social side of life. I thought I could just focus on my job and raising Ruthie and I'd be fine. But then there was that awful accident with your parents and you came home. Everything changed then. My life has been so much richer with you in it. And Ruthie already loves you so much. So I picked out a ring for you – if it's not what you want, you could exchange it.

"We've been through a lot since you came back, enough to let me know that I want you by my side. That's why I want to ask you, will you marry me?"

Tears came to Peyton's eyes and she smiled broadly.

"Oh Cameron, yes, yes, with all my heart."

He slipped the ring on her trembling finger and wrapped his arms around her in a tender hug.

"Now," he said, laying her back carefully on the pillow, "the doctor said you were to get plenty of rest and since I'm your nurse for the night, you've got to do what I say. So close those beautiful eyes and I'll wake you up in a bit. OK?"

She nodded wordlessly and kissed the side of his mouth. He drew the shades to darken the room a bit then turned to leave the room. He stopped in the doorway and looked at Peyton once more.

"I love you, Cameron."

"I love you too" he whispered, walking back to the bed for one more touch. He gave her hand a little squeeze and left Peyton's side, pulling the door closed behind him.

Chapter Thirty-Three:

A Surprise

PEYTON'S EYES WOULD NOT STAY CLOSED. AFTER CAMERON'S tender proposal, she couldn't help holding out her arm and looking at the engagement ring on her finger. Even in the dim light of the room, the sparkle of the diamond continually caught her eye. She couldn't help smiling. The smile just wouldn't go away, but eventually the tiredness returned and her eyes closed in dreamless sleep. An hour later, Cameron stuck his head in the door of her room and he whistled softly.

"Hey, sleepyhead, you doing OK?"

Peyton drew the back of her hand over her eyes and smiled involuntarily. She lifted herself on her elbows and looked at Cameron through half closed eyes.

"I'm good. What are you up to?"

"I'm going to ride back over to Greyson to make sure the fire is contained. I know Barry said the firefighters were getting it all but I just want to make sure."

"Can't you wait till later? You've been through so much."

"I won't be gone long. I just want to make sure they've gotten the fire out. I'll be right back – in time to wake you up in an hour like the doc said."

Peyton smiled weakly and waved goodbye to him, then fell back on the pillow. She listened to the sound of the ticking of the old fashioned clock on the bedside table. Its rhythmic tick-tock, tick-tock soon lulled her back to sleep. It seemed only moments later when she heard the sound of Cameron's footsteps in the next room. A smile came unbidden to her lips. She turned over on her side and looked at the door, its moldings in brilliant relief in the sunshine which came around the edges of the window shades. She watched the doorknob turn and closed her eyes pretending to sleep.

I want him to wake me up with a kiss.

When he didn't come over to the bedside, Peyton opened her eyes and saw his silhouette framed in the doorway. She waited for him to speak, then sat up quickly, too quickly as the throbbing in her head told her. Something about Cameron's silhouette wasn't right. Something was wrong, very, very wrong.

Oh my God, that's not Cameron.

Chapter Thirty-Four:

Carlos Returns

CARLOS DEL VILAR STEPPED WORDLESSLY INTO THE ROOM AND looked into Peyton's eyes, a look of pure evil in his eyes. A grin spread slowly across his face. He pulled a small revolver from his waistband and pointed it straight at her forehead. Without uttering a word, he aimed the revolver in the direction of the door. Peyton stood at his command and trembled, the pain in her head returning with a vengeance.

"What do you want from me? I don't have anythi…"

He grabbed her wrist and twisted it behind her back, forcing her to scream in agony. With the nozzle of the gun pressed firmly in her back, he shoved her toward the door. The sudden movement caused her head to throb, sending shooting pains down her back.

"You're my insurance, *chica,* "

"Cameron, help me! Cameron! Wait! No! Where are you taking me?"

Pushing her with his left hand while pressing the gun into her back, Carlos hesitated for a moment, then decided to go out the back door. At the bottom of the steps, he hit her on the back of her head just where she'd been hit before. Instantly Peyton fell to her knees and passed out. Carlos pocketed his gun and grabbed her around the waist. He threw her over his shoulder easily and headed toward his truck. Tossing her in the back seat of the cab, he threw an old blanket over her and started the engine.

Chapter Thirty-Five:
Cameron Returns to Greyson

AT GREYSON, CAMERON FOUND THE FIRE WAS INDEED OUT, though a haze still hung in the air. His nostrils were assaulted by the acrid smell of smoke. The sheriff had left several deputies there to patrol the area and assure that all was well. Firemen had stabilized the area of the house which had been affected and had marked the weakest areas of the structure with tape. The deputies on site nodded to Cameron and gave him permission to enter the grounds and cross the yellow crime scene tape. He walked around the perimeter of the house, moving his eyes from side to side in search of an errant flame, but found none. Then, using the key Peyton had given him, he entered the front hall of Greyson. He tried the light switch, but the electricity was off.

Of course. After the fire, there'd be no power.

Cameron went back out to his truck and grabbed a high powered flashlight, then took the steps two at a time. Room by room, Cameron explored the house to make sure everything was as good as it could be. He tried every window to be sure the locks were secured. He opened every closet door, lifted every curtain, and examined every corner to be sure there were no flames still unquenched. The examination took longer than he'd planned to complete. The house had a pervasive odor of smoke and some of the walls were covered in soot. It was going to take some time and money to return the house to its former glory, he realized.

Peyton's parents' bedroom was completely destroyed. Water damage was everywhere and what was not water-soaked was burned beyond recognition. It took an hour to go through the entire house. He was tired and eager to go back to Peyton but he wanted to make sure the house was as safe as it could be for Peyton. Peyton who'd just agreed to become his wife. Peyton who'd be such a wonderful mother to Ruthie. This was the least he could do for Peyton. His Peyton.

When he'd locked the door and deposited the key in his pocket, Cameron got into his truck and started the engine. A smile crossed his lips as he remembered the way Peyton had looked as he slipped the ring on her finger. She was so incredibly beautiful and good.

I've got to get back to her, he thought.

Chapter Thirty-Six:
Where's Peyton?

CAMERON DROVE BACK TOWARD HIS HOUSE AND PULLED HIS truck into the driveway of Grey's Station. He killed the engine and looked at the house, envisioning Ruthie and Peyton coming out to greet him. The sun had set and the twilight was quiet and starless. For just a minute he sat in the cab and thought about Taylor Jamison. How could a man who had once been a respected member of the community have gone so far off track? Then as he came to himself, he shuddered a bit, then emerged from the truck and walked toward the back porch of his house. When he got to the top of the steps, he stopped, a puzzled look on his face.

Why is the back door open? Pretty sure I didn't leave it this way?

Cautiously, he pushed open the door and looked inside. The house seemed to be as he'd left it. He walked down the hall to Peyton's bedroom calling her name, but there was no answer. Something was very wrong.

He looked cautiously as he turned each corner, then shouldered his way into the room where he'd left her. Seeing the empty bed, he turned and began running through the house, calling her name over and over. The bathroom, the kitchen, the living room, his bedroom – all empty. He looked out the front door, but Peyton was simply gone.

He pulled his cellphone from his back pocket and punched in 911. Within a matter of minutes, the yard was ablaze with the blue lights of half a dozen police cars. The deputies immediately began searching the area around the exterior of Cameron's house. The sheriff and another deputy came up the back stairs to begin their interior search. A technician began the process of dusting for fingerprints. Barry found Peyton's cellphone on the table by her bed and checked it for recent calls or latent fingerprints. Inside the house, Cameron walked from room to room looking for some clue to explain Peyton's disappearance, but there was none. She was just gone.

Chapter Thirty-Seven:

On the Run

CARLOS HAD TOSSED PEYTON ROUGHLY INTO THE BACK SEAT of his pickup truck and grabbed a roll of duct tape from the dash. Still unconscious from her most recent hit, Peyton flopped onto the seat. Meanwhile, Carlos pulled off a strip of tape and placed it over her mouth. Then he wrapped her wrists and ankles so that she was bound and helpless. He slammed the door, very nearly breaking her leg which was just barely inside.

Getting behind the steering wheel, he gunned the engine and took off down the lane, the tires spinning and shooting gravel everywhere.

OK now what? Where am I going to take her now?

He drove recklessly onto the highway, and then told himself to slow down.

They'll probably be looking for me soon. I don't want to draw attention to myself.

Peyton stirred in the seat beside him and groaned. She began to come to consciousness and opened her eyes. She shook her head to clear her thinking, and then winced as the pain from her second head wound hit her. She looked in cold horror at Carlos and tried unsuccessfully to scream. Her eyes opened wide as she tried to assess her situation. She struggled to a sitting position, then looked outside trying to discern her location. Carlos took his eyes off the road for a minute to look in the rear view mirror at his captive.

"You will need to be very good, *chica,* and maybe you'll come out of this ok."

"Ummpfh! Ummpfh!"

"What's that? I can't quite understand you. You'll have to speak up, *chica.* You see, things haven't gone exactly as I had planned. So we're on to plan B. This is the part where I use you as my bargaining chip. You're kind of my Get out of Jail Free card."

Carlos pulled the truck into a secluded dirt road off the highway and silenced the engine. Turning to Peyton, he put his index finger to his lips and whispered,

"Now here is what's going to happen. I'm going to take the tape off your lips. Then I'm going to hold my cellphone up to your ear and you're going to talk to your boyfriend. You're going to tell him you're OK but that your *amigo* Carlos needs a little money and a safe ride out of the country. Understand?"

Peyton nodded her head, her heart pounding, her eyes wide open now. She cringed against the door.

"No funny stuff now."

Waving his gun, he said, "Because I've got my little friend here in case you get crazy. OK?"

Peyton nodded again and moaned as Carlos ripped the tape from her mouth.

"Now *chica,* tell me the number."

Her mind refused to work. She struggled to remember Cameron's cellphone number, and then pulled it from her memory bank.

Carlos punched the numbers and held the phone to her ear.

"Hello? Who is this?"

Peyton closed her eyes as she heard the sweet sound of Cameron's voice.

"Cameron, it's me. Help me. The copperheads…"

"Peyton, where are you? Are you all right?"

"Cam…"

Carlos snatched the phone from her ear and grinned. He held it to his ear and whispered into the mouthpiece.

"Listen, *gringo,* I'm gonna say this just once. I've got your girl and if you want her back, I'm gonna need transportation out of the country – with NO police presence anywhere. I also need a little running money – say, a half million? I'll call back in half an hour. Think about it."

He punched the button to close the call and grinned at Peyton. Then with the back of his hand, he slapped her cheek hard. Her head bounced against the window glass and she began to whimper.

Chapter Thirty-Eight:

The Search

CAMERON AND SHERIFF BARRY JAMES WALKED NERVOUSLY back and forth in the small parlor of Grey's Station. Cameron had just gotten off the phone from talking to Sue, who had confirmed that Ruthie had been eager to come home to her daddy. When he told her about Peyton's abduction, Sue gasped and told him she'd keep Ruthie safe.

"Thanks, Sue. It means a lot to me. I don't know if there's anyone else to look out for, but just in case, I'll feel safer if Ruthie stays with you. And keep all three of the kids close at home. I don't know how much these guys know about my family. Can Charlie work from home today?"

"Don't worry, Cam. He's right here beside me. And he's not going anywhere."

At least that's one thing I don't have to worry about.

No sooner had he closed the call than the phone rang. Cameron immediately pushed the button to answer and heard the terrified voice of Peyton.

"Cameron, it's me. Help me. The copperheads…"

"Peyton, where are you? Are you all right?"

"Cam…"

Suddenly Cameron heard the lowered voice of Carlos Del Vilar. Immediately he went into high alert. He picked up a pencil and began jotting notes on a pad on the desk. After the hang-up, Cameron rubbed his forehead with his palm and paced back and forth in his living room. Sheriff Barry James stood up from the desk where he'd been talking to his dispatcher. He ran his fingers through his thinning grey hair and looked at Cameron, concern written all over his face.

"OK, man, what is it? What'd he say?"

" It's Carlos – he's got Peyton. Said he'd call back in thirty minutes but he needed a half million dollars and safe transport out of the country. Barry, we've got to find her. But he said no police presence. What do we do?"

"We've got to get a location on him so let's trace him.

Cameron paced the floor, stopping periodically to look out the window. In a tall pine across the river behind his house, a bald eagle circled, then lit on the topmost branch. In his beak, he held the body of a limp snake. Cameron's mind went back to a day months ago when he watched the eagle's nest through his binoculars. Absentmindedly, he picked up the binoculars and trained them on the tree. His mind traveled back to the day he first took Peyton to The Refuge. Suddenly he threw down the binoculars and turned.

"Barry! Come on! I think I know where they are."

Chapter Thirty-Nine:
Tenant House

THE SHERIFF FOLLOWED CAMERON OUT THE FRONT DOOR yelling to his deputies to follow him. Cameron told the sheriff where to drive and Barry headed his Crown Victoria away from the house, lights flashing and siren blaring. Barry gunned the high powered engine. The tires sprayed gravel as the car spun out onto the highway, followed by six other sheriff's department cars all headed a few miles away to the tenant house Cameron had shown Peyton so long ago.

"When I showed her the Refuge right after she came home from London," Cameron told the sheriff breathlessly, "I told her to be careful where she walked because I had seen a copperhead around there. When she called me just now, she said something odd. It sounded like she was worried about copperheads. It didn't make sense then, but it just hit me. She was talking in code. That has to be where he's taken her."

Barry took his eyes off the road for a minute and looked at Cameron. He pressed his foot even harder on the accelerator pedal and looked straight ahead grimly.

A minute later, Barry turned down a dark dirt road in the middle of a field. He signaled to the other police cars to turn off their sirens and lights. He slowed the car to a stop in front of the tenant house and eased out.

Cameron and the deputies followed suit and hunkered down behind a wall of police cruisers lined up around the old house. Ducking his head, Barry yelled toward the shack.

"Carlos! Let's do this the easy way. Let the girl go and we'll talk about a reduced sentence for you."

Ping! A bullet bounced off the car above Cameron's shoulder.

"It came from the house. Stay down, everybody," Barry yelled. "Peyton, are you all right? Peyton? Can you hear me?"

There was no answer. Then suddenly, a plaintive sob came from inside.

"Cameron, help me!" Peyton cried.

Carlos held her in front of him as he stood in front of the window.

"Hey, cowboy. You want her back? You better tell your buddy the cop to let me go. I already had a piece of her. She's fine, brother."

"OK, Carlos, we're leaving. Just don't hurt her."

"Too thin, brother. I need my insurance. She's coming with me."

Barry and Cameron whispered a minute to each other. In the background, they heard the muffled sobs of Peyton coming from the window. Cameron hunkered down further and began crawling on all fours behind the line of police cars circling the house.

"OK, Carlos. We're pulling out," Barry yelled, watching carefully as Cameron moved. "We're leaving a patrol car here for you. Key's in the ignition. I just talked to the Governor's office. There'll be a private jet waiting for you at the Leesburg airfield near Dulles with instructions to fly you wherever you want to go. They're putting together the money right now. It should be on the plane by the time you get there. You can leave the girl at the airfield. But this all goes away if Peyton is hurt. You hear?"

There was silence again and then Carlos appeared in front of the window, holding Peyton by the hair, a gun pointed to her temple.

"I'm waiting, Sheriff, but not for long."

One by one the sheriff and his deputies drove away in their cars, leaving one behind as they had promised. Soon the field was quiet again. Inside the house, Carlos still trained his gun on Peyton whose wrists and ankles were bound with duct tape. He lay down his gun and picked up the roll of duct tape to cover her mouth.

In just the time it took to lay down his handgun and cover Peyton's mouth with another strip of duct tape, the sound of glass breaking interrupted the silence. Carlos looked up and saw Cameron lunging at him from a window in the back of the room. A mad scramble for the pistol ensued with Cameron kicking it out of Carlos's reach. Carlos's hands went around Cameron's neck but he broke free, grabbed one of Carlos's hands and forced it behind him.

Peyton inched backwards against the wall watching helplessly in horror as the fight continued at her feet. She tried to scream but the duct tape held so her screams were muffled.

Carlos broke free once more from Cameron's grasp and reached for the gun which was now within his grasp. Training it on Cameron, he tossed the roll of duct tape to him.

"Ok, Hero. Tape your ankles together. I'll tell you when to stop. Do it, or you both get it."

Cameron did as he was ordered, looking all the while into Peyton's eyes.

"Are you OK, Peyton?" he said, breathlessly.

She nodded, with a look of terror in her eyes as Carlos grabbed up the tape and proceeded to shackle Cameron's wrists together.

"Sorry there's no room for your boyfriend but I only have two tickets."

He kicked Cameron in the shin and cut the tape from Peyton's ankles so she could walk to the cruiser. Pushing her along in front of him, he pressed the nose of the gun into the small of her back. She looked back at Cameron who nodded to her, offering silent comfort as she left.

Carlos opened the back door and pushed his hostage into the rear, slamming the door quickly. He opened the door and leaned in to get into the driver's seat. Without warning, he was knocked to the ground.

Ping! Ping! Two bullets from the high powered rifle of a police marksman found their target and Carlos fell to the ground instantly. Inside the car, Peyton tried to scream under the duct tape but she was as trapped as ever. *Please, God. Please let Cameron be safe.*

Soon, however, the sound of police sirens approaching let her know that her ordeal was nearly over. The sheriff's car skidded to a stop next to the cruiser he had left for Carlos, whose lifeless body lay stretched out alongside the car. Barry got out of the car and opened the back door, releasing Peyton from her bonds. She rubbed her wrists and ankles to bring the blood back into them.

"In the house. Hurry. He has Cameron tied up in there."

"Are you all right?"

"Yes! Yes! Please! See about Cameron!"

A few moments later, a deputy walked beside Cameron, his arm supporting the released captive whose legs were still uncertain. As soon as he saw Peyton, however, he ran to her side and took her in his arms.

"Cameron, thank God."

She buried her face into his shoulder and cried, "Thank God you're all right. Thank God."

Chapter Forty:

The End

BACK AT GREY'S STATION, PEYTON LEANED BACK IN Cameron's recliner. The sheriff had insisted that both Cameron and Peyton be checked out in the hospital, so he had sent the two of them in an ambulance to Inova Loudoun's state of the art emergency room. There, a team of medical personnel, who had been alerted to their arrival ahead of time, waited to examine them.

The physicians inspected their bruises and cleaned and bandaged their abrasions. The attending physician gave them bottles of painkillers for the throbbing that would come and released them. Barry drove them back to Cameron's, telling them that he'd make regular patrols around the house for the next few days, just in case.

"Thank you, buddy," Cameron said, extending his hand to Barry. "I owe you my life. It was foolish to try to sneak around behind the house the way I did. I just had to try something, though. Which one of your deputies was the sharpshooter?"

"Guess that was me," the sheriff replied. I took a chance on coming back to The Refuge on that other lane and hoped he wouldn't hear me. When I got in range, I killed the engine and waited. When I saw Carlos come out with just Peyton, I was scared but I knew I had to act. So I took the shot and got lucky. It could have gone the other way so easily."

Peyton tried to rise from the chair, then thought better of it and sank back into the cushions.

"Barry – we owe you our lives. Thank you just isn't enough."

"You can make it up to me. The Police Retirement Fundraiser's coming up."

He grinned, tipped his hat and left. Cameron went back over to Peyton and took her carefully into his strong, muscled arms.

"I thought I'd never hold you again. It almost killed me. Thank God you're all right. "

Peyton closed her eyes and rested her head on his shoulder.

"I'm never leaving."

Epilogue:

The Christmas House Tour

CAMERON WAS DRESSED IN HIS BEST TAN KHAKIS AND WORE a red sweater over a white oxford cloth button down shirt. Peyton, wearing a black and red plaid dress and black flats was fussing over Ruthie's hair. Ruthie, wearing a pair of green corduroy overalls and turtleneck shirt underneath was squirming.

"Ow, no more, Mommy," she said as Peyton struggled to put the last barrette in her hair. I wanna watch the parade on TV."

"But don't you want to look nice for the Christmas House Tour, Sweetie?"

Finally, she snapped the last barrette in place and Ruthie scampered off to sit beside her cousins Will and Noah. Sue and Charlie had brought them over to stay at Greyson while Peyton and Cameron played host at The Refuge.

After the fire at Greyson and her abduction by Carlos, Peyton had stayed at Cameron's house for several weeks while waiting for information from her insurance agent. Except for the center hall staircase, the fire damage was smaller than originally thought, so they replaced the roof, waterproofed the basement, repointed the brick where necessary, and replaced the staircase exactly as it had been. Luckily Peyton's family photographs gave the restoration team lots of visuals to work from. Peyton and Cameron were able to move back into Greyson with Ruthie immediately after their September wedding. Cameron and Peyton moved into the brand new master suite while Ruthie was given a room of her own next door.

Sue and Ruthie had been Peyton's only wedding attendants and Charlie had stood beside Cameron as best man. Noah and Will had both served as ring bearers and argued the entire length of the wedding aisle as to who was carrying their pillow better. Chub and Emmaline had catered a simple feast for after the wedding. Sarah and Walter and their grandchildren had attended the wedding with Dusty in a trailer nearby. All the children were looking forward to having a ride on the pony after the ceremony. Dusty tirelessly gave Ruthie, Sarah and Walter's grandchildren, Noah and Will rides up and down the lane. Dr. Livesay, the physician who treated Peyton after the initial kidnapping was another guests and brought her three children and husband as well.

The wedding had been held under the shade of the twenty oak trees of the Refuge whose future was now ensured. In fact, Cameron had taken on the restoration of the Refuge as kind of a pet project, one which was giving him great personal satisfaction. The rooms of the great old house were slowly coming to life again.

Taylor had been arrested immediately upon being apprehended and, along with the other men involved, had been imprisoned in the Loudoun County Jail for weeks before and after their court trials. They were awaiting their sentencing date which was set for the week after Christmas. Carlos, of course, had died at the scene of the capture at the tenant house.

Slowly, life returned to its usual slow pace. As summer moved into fall, Cameron began the process of harvesting and putting by his crops. He had taken only a day or two off to marry Peyton, promising a honeymoon during the winter. Peyton agreed so long as Ruthie went with them.

"She's had enough to deal with. We shouldn't leave her behind," Peyton insisted and Cameron concurred.

As soon as the crops from Greyson were harvested in the weeks after his wedding, Cameron had begun the process of making the Refuge beautiful again. Beginning the reclamation of the Refuge could not start, though, until he removed the jungle of honeysuckle, poison ivy and weeds lining the front gates as well as removing any dead or diseased trees throughout the property. He graded both roads leading to the Refuge and spread gravel over them, creating a much smoother approach to the house. Then he'd hired an army of craftsmen and workers to re-roof the entire building, re-plaster and paint the woodwork inside and out. Cameron found the original shutters in one of the outbuildings still in their original green paint color. He had them restored and re-installed on all the windows. One group of workmen installed copper gutters on the house while another shored up the stable, smokehouse, and various other outbuildings.

The workers re-glazed all the windows, ensuring the wavy glass panes were carefully placed back in the windows Then they began the installation of central heat and air systems, careful to make them as inconspicuous as possible. Workmen suspended on scaffolding labored to replace rotting 18th century crown molding. The few pieces of furniture which had been left in the house were in surprisingly good shape after a coat of lemon oil had been applied. The crocheted netting over the bed was cleaned and repaired. Peyton searched online and found bed coverings that looked surprisingly like the old quilts which had rotted. Peyton and Cameron had worked day after day during the first weeks of November, polishing the old house until it gleamed. The heart pine floors had been given a coat of wax and a new chandelier had been installed in the dining room. The broken mirror glass had been repaired with a new beveled mirror glass replacement. A few missing banister railings were found under a muslin sheet in the living room and were reinstalled.

The Pepto-Bismol pink paint had been removed and the banisters were now back to their original wood.

The work on the interior was still ongoing but the whole building smelled delightfully of polish and balsam. A work of this magnitude took time. So for days, the couple walked from room to room making adjustments, making notes of things that were still needed and simply looking at the grand old house in admiration.

Now The Refuge was to be on the annual Loudoun County Christmas house tour. The mansion was not finished by a long shot, but Peyton and Cameron's friends had urged them to show their home anyway. So Cameron had installed sod along the drive which made a magnificent approach. The property looked beautiful with tents set up on the lawn underneath the oaks. Local charities set up their displays under the tents and their representatives looked forward to enriching their coffers. Cameron and Peyton donated the entire amount of entrance fees collected for the house tour to the hospital which had treated them.

Peyton looked admiringly at Ruthie as she sat in front of the television with her cousins. Reaching for her husband's hand, she said a silent prayer of thanks for her blessings.

"Have fun today with Aunt Sue and the boys," Peyton said, picking up Ruthie and giving her a hug, "Daddy and I will be home soon."

"OK Squirt, make sure you show Will and Noah how to play basketball up in the ballroom," Cameron said. He grabbed Ruthie, swung her around and set her back down. Cameron had hung a Nerf basketball hoop in the ballroom on the third floor and marked off the foul lines on the floor with painter's tape. It had become one of their favorite places to play.

Cameron and Peyton got in the truck for the short drive over to the Refuge. They looked out at the verdant pastures surrounding Greyson and the fields beyond the fences. The corn and soybeans had been harvested and the rows were bare. Each of the barns and sheds at Greyson had been hung with large fir wreaths in honor of the season. The fences lining the lane were hung with yards of thick cedar roping.

The morning was brisk and cold with the promise of a light snowfall later in the day. The ride to the Refuge took barely fifteen minutes. Since Cameron had graded the lane, the ruts were gone. The brick pillars at the end of the lane had been repointed and hung with greenery. A new wooden sign of dark green letters on a cream colored board identified "The Refuge." To anyone driving a car through the double lane of oaks, the freshly painted Refuge was framed magnificently. Peyton and Cameron had hung a huge wreath of boxwood on the porch railing above the front door. Cascades of pine roping marked the outline of the porch and the door frame below.

Inside the center hall, Peyton had decorated a grand Fraser fir in a simple, old fashioned style – tiny white lights, ropes of popcorn and cranberries, and bows of red ribbon. At the top of the tree was a star, cut from a piece of tin. Candles set inside hurricane lanterns and greenery were set about throughout the house. The wide boards of the heart pine floors throughout the house gleamed from the lemon oil that Peyton and Cameron had applied. A brisk fire was going in the parlor's ornate marble fireplace, comforting on this 30 degree day. Cameron had made certain to have the chimneys cleaned and inspected before having fires there. He grabbed a fireplace poker and gave the logs a stir, then swept some fallen embers back into the firebox. Red ribbon bows were cheery punctuation marks scattered everywhere. Other than the dining table and the beds upstairs, there were few pieces of furniture in the rooms – Cameron and Peyton both felt that for the purposes of the house tour, the emptiness was a plus.

Cameron and Peyton set to work in the makeshift kitchen preparing the punch and coffee. The new kitchen would be added after the holidays but wiring and plumbing had already been completed. Cameron set out trays of cookies and finger foods surrounding a topiary of boxwood and Lady apples, but couldn't resist snagging just one.

"Just a taste test, you know," he grinned mischievously.

Peyton made one last pass with the dust cloth over the stair railing and looked around her with pleasure. The house, practically devoid of furniture, was elegant in its simplicity.

"Its emptiness kind of leaves room for the imagination to take over, don't you think?" Peyton said, smiling and wrapping her arms around her husband's waist.

"It was beautiful before, but now, it's really hard to describe the change – it's even more wonderful."

"I think that's because the house knows it's loved again. It truly is a refuge."

Peyton looked out the sidelights of the front door and saw car after car heading toward the house. The Refuge was to be the first stop on the Christmas house tour. After the tour when the renovations were complete, the house and grounds were to be leased to the Boys' and Girls' Clubs of Leesburg as a learning center, therapeutic riding program and campground. It had been Cameron's idea to help the charity that had been so much help to Sue and him in their teen years. Peyton gave Cameron another hug and looked up into his blue eyes.

"You know, I think I know how the house feels today."

"I can't believe how lucky I am," he replied. "A year ago, it was just Ruthie and me. Now, I feel like I'll never be lonely again."

Cameron smiled, winked and kissed the top of his wife's head and together they opened the front door to receive their guests.

The End